TWELVE AGAIN

by Terry Holt

M.O.R.E. Publishers

St. Louis, MO

M.O.R.E. Publishers Corp.

P.O. Box 38285

St. Louis, MO 63138

Printed in the United States

ISBN 978-0-9820354-0-5

THoltArtist@Hotmail.com

Dedicated to my family
who kept me out of trouble,
and helped me to be the man
that I am today.

TWELVE AGAIN

TABLE OF CONTENTS

CHAPTER 1:
NEIGHBORHOOD GANG

By the time I was ten I began to realize that not only did my shoes matter but they kind of made me who I was. So when I looked at my plain white prowling, it kept me in touch with the fact that I couldn't rely on my style to get me connected to the "in crowd". I began to feel as If I had to improve my personality to compete with the hype crowd. Therefore the beginning of my life was one so very, very, low key.

Walking home from our elementary school wasn't just a walk. This was the plank that you would be made to walk, that is if this were a pirate's boat, so to speak. In these walks to the house, you'd be shown up if you were scared or if you were brave. All the same, the next day would be one of cheer or a long week of shame.

Our house was the yellow one on the corner. In the so familiar street to our house, I followed my brother from behind. We had been living there in that house now since I began the first grade, and this neighborhood knew of one way to interact. That was aggressively.

The bell rang out. Everyone under four feet tall and full of adrenaline - the ones who sat only seconds ago motionless, jumped to their inner instinct and hit the playground swings first. On our playground, the ones who could soar the highest and spin the most were indeed qualified to boast that they were the latest cartoon super heroes.

Each of us was a miniature miracle. None of us knew about the way to be just who we were. Only we knew we had to be known by the nearest girls in our class. So, out of all of the many things that could be done to impress a girl, not really knowing much, we got our smiles and punches by performance of some of the most ridiculous measures known to child kind.

Anyway, two seats in front of me sat the cutest girl since Vanity was a young girl. Yet, upon each instance of eye contact between me and yet a significant other, I repeatedly chose to shy away, to some other object in sight.

My heart was pumping pure passion, every morning, with every walk to the pencil sharpener, and with every game of seven up. All of these were my golden opportunities to exchange what I felt were "You know, we should be a couple" sort of glances.

Sure enough, as much as I might have prepared at home, never were the approaches as smooth and coordinated in public. They were always incomplete sentences, always overacted or just straight foolish gestures of what I presumed to be the proper interaction, with whom an attraction was sought. However, lo and behold, still I had the advantage over my crew.

The one we all were blown over, just happened to stay three streets down from mine, plus I had a friend, so to speak, that just so happened to stay across the street from her. Ya dig? I began to feel the rush of the thrill of these last weeks of the school year. I smiled, knowing that I'd need shade during those long anticipated strolls.

On a Saturday, oh yeah, it was definitely going down. My older brother was, to me, like a technique guide to the outside world. He knew the arts and crafts of making bows and arrows that actually had range and accuracy. He also knew how to make spears, boomerangs - the works.

This particular morning, we all met up at the old house on the end of the corner. The base was the roof of the house itself. There we would strategize about the latest idea of wolf hunting at the all famous "gravel pit". From this point, things would be pretty much on a more dangerous scale, for these outside animals were real. We all were either from 9 to 12 years of age, and well armed with bows and arrows.

Our journey began with the trail off the main street of which is Holmes Road. Along this particular street, we rode our bikes up and down the concrete hills in search of the path into the plains of the wooded area. There would be the beginning of our journey.

"Aye yawl, we probably need to be on the look out," was heard once we left the main street, bracing ourselves. The terrain was about to take a turn for the worst! The "gravel pit" was nothing more than a small lake about a few acres back behind the woods. The path was very steep at times, meaning at the bottom. We usually got off the bikes and pushed them up the incline. After ten minutes of this procedure, the lake could be seen and all the way up to it, there were woods on every side. Along the side of this semi-dried out lake were paw prints. They could be seen all about the area. Some disappeared into the brush that was seen only a few meters away.

"Yawl think we gonna see what left the prints here?" one of our closer friends of the street said amongst us. We had our weapons. As crude as they appeared to be, they also could be quite dangerous in the right hands. After 15 minutes of surveillance, we thought it was best to depart, plus the fact that those footprints actually meant that we should probably be getting kind of like out of those woods for now.

The next school day I sat idle in my seat for I had a secret. I had a big pocket full of now-n-laters, and not one intention of sharing the least. With several hours to go until lunch, and this being the English part of the day, this secret was vital to my very survival, I had assumed.

First, perfecting the art of making the least noise as possible was a sport to me. I'd take one hand, place it in my pocket, and then unfold each candy fold one at a time. If my secret stash had been perceived by an onlooker, there was sure to be suspiciousness about our area and alerting the teacher to the mischief about the room. Then in doing so, this would be hindering me from the only thing that a child hid before there was any money in the pockets.

There the teacher stood in her heels, stockings, and long dress with the blouse to match the shoes, and glasses. She was good looking and I found out that she had a very good nose. Anyway, there the teacher was looking at me suspiciously! After calling me to the desk, she let me know quietly that I'd be sitting with them in the shade while the others played. Still I got to keep my candy for I was an "A" student!

CHAPTER 2:
THE BICYCLE

The boy's house was now in sight. I could see from the top of the hill that there his bike was, with no other around. I continued until I had finally made it to the house. I only had to walk past the driveway, up to the very bike that he himself owned. Under extreme frustration, along with being paranoid, I indiscriminately took his bike to the street – and then began to destroy it!

It wasn't ong before someone detected my intrusion. It could have been the noise or just the very public display of rage itself that captured the unsuspecting household's attention in such a short time. The door opened and the suspected thief was soon closing in on me with the look of disbelief at what he was witnessing.

He cried out, "Hey...hey...why ya destroying my bike?" I heard him, but at the same time, I didn't; for the rage was intensely high!

"You stole my bike. You said it ya self!" I managed to convey that to him while all the time, stomping the front and back wheels.

With the tears and cries mixed with the sincerity of his voice, I began to feel remorse as in one would feel after making some unfixable mistake. I began to wonder if I should have at least looked around before coming to a conclusion. I felt bad about what I had just done to his bike with him being innocent and all. However, now my focus rested on whom it really was that had gotten me. I was determined to get to the bottom of this 'cause I was going to walk the whole 'hood and question to the where about of my bike.

The fact that my other friends still had their vehicles made the situation more drastic for me to grasp. All I knew for sure was that it was going to be trouble for which ever it was. Nonetheless, with nothing more to accomplish at the present scene I walked back down the hill half-heartedly.

I woke late on the next morning. After adjusting my eyes to the day, there was no interest what so ever in the television. My collection of solders and Indians didn't even receive my attention, for that particular day.

I found myself thinking about how I was almost a good stunt rider on the bike. Then I kept thinking a bit longer about the injuries that came along with the stunts, and about the dangers of "shut-eye" riding. I made it to eight at one time before I ran into a parked car. I limped a few days and bled a little bit. Maybe, I thought to myself, it probably would be better off to use my feet for a while.

Along with that was the fact that I rather neglected my closest neighbors. With the appearance of a nice day ahead I walked to Toni's house. Upon seeing him already outside I yelled, "Hey ya wanna walk over to Ira's house; play some Nintendo, or something?"

In the midst of my questions I couldn't help but notice his pre-occupation of observing an almost ancient relic of a van. He had an uncle that saw fit to leave it there in the yard, give, or take five or six years ago. Dust and leaves covered the bluish-gray faded paint. The tires were almost flat. One of the small side windows was shattered, but still it stood as one structure.

We pretty much considered it junk. After peering through the weathered windows, it was presumed safe enough to climb inside.

"I'm uh gonna drive like this here when I get old enough, straight down and low in the seats like a true Mac," I said while adjusting my small structure to suit my position.

However, after another minute or so of jumping around, the window that was shattered began to break down, falling by pieces onto the seats and floor.

"Man...dog...my uncle gonna kill us man!" Tonio said while laughing all at the same time.

"Man...this junk?   He probably don't even want it."

We both agreed, considering the amount of time it had been there. Thus, for now, the destruction would really begin. After growing weary with the filth and confines of the rusted thing, we got out of it. Thenceforth we climbed on top of the vehicle instead.

"Hey, man, you can see the whole hood from up here," he said after being on top for a second more than I.   There were rocks lying nearby, and we could see other children playing the worst of what they considered basketball. Suddenly the vehicle's hood began to give in, so we in turn jumped off. The rocks that were at our reach gave initiative for target practice. "Might as well break the rest of the windows we thought." For us it seemed like it would be fun enough.

All I know is that I was just getting ready to sit back and watch whatever was on the television. Then from the background arises one of the softest knocks I had ever heard radiating from the front door. "Who is it?"

I opened the door to see standing there Tonio himself twitching, stuttering, and all teary eyed.

"What's up? " I cautiously asked of him. I began to feel the awareness sequence of upcoming   disciplinary   actions   in   the atmosphere.

"My uncle. He wanna' see you. He mad at us 'cause we broke his windows. He wants yo' momma to give him some money for 'em."

The adrenaline, plus the tingling, now began to rush up and down my neck and back. For inside, I knew that this was the situation that called for the leatherness, of a belt that my siblings and I knew very well. It was time to leave my house now really, before the news spread inside.

"Man, them windows was already broke. We just knocked the rest of the pieces out," I said standing there guilty.

I looked behind me as I stepped out of the door to see my mom, my sisters, and my brother. The TV was tuned to the Cosby show. They seemed to be at so much peace. There was so much relaxation. In fact they were at ease.

On the other hand, there I stood trembling, afraid, expecting the worst, and looking into the face of what I was about to become.

"Um I may just walk down there and tell him that I'm sorry or some' n."

"We can ask if we can work it off." I thought desperately and searchingly. I would have to come up with something - anything besides having to tell my Mom that he was demanding money for the damage that we had caused his vehicle. I thought about school tomorrow, and about how I would get through the day. It was about a ten-minute walk, but to me it took about ten seconds.

I could see his family in the front yard, and there stood a tall sort of fat, bushy-haired man with a hat pulled down low, and in the front-part of his face was a beard and mustache. He had on a "hell of an attitude." All of this I noticed four houses away!

It didn't occur to me that I had a compensation for courage - horror. I think everything in me was telling me to hide. Yet I knew that I was far too late. So with every step afterwards, words of excuse and manipulation poured into my cranium, for I was lost and far away from the land of ease of which I was in not more than twenty minutes ago!

Now I was within paces before I was in actual conversation range. My eyes sparkled with the tears of fear and uncertainty.

"I'm telling you to go back home and tell ya momma to come see me about paying me for them windows in that there van...," he said to me.

Whatever kind of story I had in mind still couldn't erase the fact that most definitely there wasn't going to be a happy ending to this night. I turned around and walked off shaking. Now as I closed in on our house, it dawned on me that now was the time in between what I remember as cause and effect. This equaled out to our mistakes earlier this week.

I thought about the many times when I'd

gotten myself into similar situations. Then I decided that it was better to go on ahead and get over with punishment. I jogged through our lawn and up the porch steps. On into the front door I went.

I noticed that the favorite show was still on and that everyone was in good spirits. There I was twitching and looking rather uneasy. I might as well have worn a red flag. There was just too much nervousness that was about to be displaying amongst a most unsuspecting family.

There I was, a splitting-image of what I looked like every time I was about to get the beat down. The eyes were watery and searching for safety as hands and arms were in places where the strikes usually began. I was prepared for today's administration of discipline

"But man," I thought, "this here has got to stop."

Into the kitchen I walked as I heard the sounds of supper being prepared, thus alerting me to the fact that my mom would be seeing me very soon anyway. After looking into the refrigerator, the camouflage of discreetness was wearing off fast. Therefore, it seemed better to take a seat at the table.

"Mom, this dude down the street gotta car in the backyard and me and my friend accidentally knocked out one of the small, side windows."

She might have heard me or maybe she

didn't. I got no immediate reply. Maybe this was a good time to add another detail for our defenses,

"The car isn't running...it's a junk car...hasn't worked in the longest time."

"He talking about he wants you to pay for some of the damage?"

After those words, I noticed a change in the air, for I had spoken the forbidden language of a child's misconduct. This brought about some money ordeal.

"Well at least it came out well," I thought while I sat there and waited for the quietness to end. Anything would do, for I was in full suspense!

She was a bit surprised at me, for what I told her of the situation. However, it was pretty much the truth. All of the above said was what I had planned to tell. The outcome changed the very way I saw things as a young child.

My mother pretty much was like "The hell with what's his face!" She hadn't even the least consideration about what he thought was owed. With that being the response, there was no beating, nor punishment, just the image of her in my mind being on my side. It felt good to be in the clear after suffering from such mental anguish, even though it didn't appear so. I really hated those times when I was caught anyway in-spite of the half lies.

CHAPTER 3:
THE BROKEN GLASS

What I witnessed and took onto the next day was a lesson. The lesson was that if someone had anger against you, then it was on you to either surrender to pressure, or become a joke among your peers. On-the-other hand, you could enhance your own pressure.

I admired my mom's attitude and decision concerning the other day's problem. She wasn't budging the least. At-that-point in my life, at the tender age of which I was - I knew I would live to that code. I knew that I would do damage though. Yet I knew that I could be wrong in many cases. I only felt that now when it came down to confrontation, I wouldn't be the one bowing down trembling and afraid. I would be the pursuer of such drama!

All I could think to myself while sitting idle on the porch was "Be no punk for no one - not the bees, nor the dogs that ran around in packs." Neither would the bullies deter me from the way I had set out to live.

I slept better later that night. Images of cartoons really were bubbling in my soul. As I awoke, I realized that it was Friday morning and we just so happened to have a test! I never sweated that though. I figured out during my earlier years in school that if I wanted to draw a picture that stood a chance for me to keep, I had better finish my assignment.

Growing to this procedure was to me a gift if I had ever seen one. This process allowed me to finish my work and even have time left for the completion of my pictures - anything to capture attention when I could!

To my immediate right sat one of the fellas that I myself had boxed with at least a few dozen times. I could read his lips as he held his fist into my sight. I knew that once we were allowed to use the restroom, a fight would be going on.

I laughed with joy knowing in my mind that I would get the pleasure of boxing with an opponent that had been known to go a few rounds. We all appreciated the value of soldier-ship and we weren't just going to box with any Joe who did not know the game. At the times when we encountered the real boxers, we could tell the Joes easily. They usually were the ones up against the walls getting their lights punched out.

We all exchanged the "I got the best of you" kind of looks. Nevertheless, in truth, we all had a mutual feeling of soldier-ship.

With no more than a couple of hours left in the school day, I mentally began to format an evening for myself. I had the option of either taking advantage of my opportunity to spend the evening with my most admired neighbor down the street, or I could meet up with the fellas for another escapade of nightlife chaos. Choosing the first was to me a sweeter deal.

As I said before, people never really knew me for my wardrobe. So I could be seen that day on my stroll, with the white tennis shoes, the brown straight leg jeans, and the faded blue T-shirt. I thought to myself about the awkwardness of me knocking on the door of a classmate that I really didn't even kick it with like that. I wondered if anyone would notice.

Today was a rather warm day. It was warmer than my wind jacket and jeans. Therefore, I did best in the attire I selected.

I had a habit of tossing stones, so every suitable rock I came across became the ammunition I needed for a distant stop sign, a mailbox, the streetlight, - whatever seemed appropriate. I tossed a stone at the street sign that read STOP. I kept missing it by more than a few feet.

Sensing the inaccuracy, I kept an eye out for yet another selection. I spotted a bottle hidden away in the shrubs along the side of the street. I really could just chunk the rock and chances were that I would hit one of the many bottles that lined the side of our street. "There were many beer drinkers," I thought to myself. "Beer smells so nasty." I could never imagine myself ever drinking a beer. "The mixtures smelled as if they could pass for something other than one would drink," I thought in disgust. Yet and still, beer was a very familiar sight at our house at times, during a party.

Now this is what I called a day after school. As I approached the street that I knew so well, one could begin to hear the voices of the kids that were recognizable from that street. It seemed as if they were all chattering about who was the one who would do the best on the final class exam. It was time for me to make an introduction.

"Wus up y'all? Wus going on?"

The looks that I got in return were welcoming. There stood London, Shakita, Tameka, Kevin, and their newest neighbor, Alicia. Kevin spoke first saying "You probably ain't even worried about the tests are you, Bro, since you smart and all in classes?"

He continued, "Matter of fact, I need to sit by you and maybe help myself a little bit here and there. Hunh?"

I thought to myself for a second about

the content of his statement. Then I regained focus on the three girls who stood amongst us. I could smell the gum, and I could see their ponytails. I could see their marble beads and freshly permed hair. I found myself thinking that I wouldn't mind if they sat around me for those three hours of test time. One could just imagine the looks that we would sneak to each other; the smiles; the acknowledgment of how boring the stories were in the textbook; how we noticed each other's mistakes; the earthquake of erasing; and the low sound of tuba notes.

"Hey Lenell, what cha 'bout to do anyway?" London asked of me.

"Well I was around the corner and I wanted to see if y'all wanted to go up to the playground with me."

"Wus up?"

I could tell by the vibe that they weren't trying to leave this area at all. Then I began noticing the disapproving looks they cast at me at times, as if to say my welcome was wearing thin. My temper was aroused a little bit, but I decided to settle this rather peacefully by not fanning their smoke into flames. Besides, the new girl would think that we were showing off.

When there was a slight distraction amongst the girls, I asked my homeboy, about the new girl. The response made me know that this was considered sacred property of some sort, as for the fellows that looked out for any sucker's luck.

My friends turned to walk with me. Our

walk began along the inclined street. Familiar houses saluted me from small pieces of the past, brought to light as I glanced at them. He hesitated before answering straight out.

"She is not even like the girls we are use to man. She'll choose somebody probably toward the time of graduation and stuff, maybe on a field trip or what not. She'll say she looking for somebody cool or sunning like that."

What came across to the ears was no more than cheap disguise and straight smoke. They all wanted her to themselves.

"Hold up y'all. Let's go back down with 'em for a lil' while," I exclaimed.

"Man you always falling for them type dude. Why don't you just let her look around first," said London, the older one of us.

"Um," thinking to myself. "Now, first of all, total language used just now was nothing more than fighting words in my ears. Feeling myself losing patience with the two goons, I wondered if they were showing off.

I walked on ahead of the two chumps. They were standing around watching each other grow old while I was thinking more like, "Hey, let's go on back over and conversate a while longer." We could make the songs that we hear on the radio much more appreciated. At least, at this point, I appreciated music more now that I was close to the tender age of thirteen. Maybe the steps between us got shorter, for I really did not have anything sensible to say to the quote unquote "new girl."

"You Alicia?" I asked of her once she perceived I was entirely too close to just merely stand there in silence. She didn't have time to respond, for her girlfriends spoke up for her. I guessed anyway.

"She already got a boyfriend and he's in the seventh grade."

Was it me or was it that all of a sudden no one on the street here? Had I really been too comfortable with my presence today?

"Damn. What in the world has this new girl started around here?" My old friends are acting shady with me. Then my partner's next-door neighbor gotta slick anger against me. So I eventually told them, "I'll just...uh...catch up later on...perhaps tomorrow." The friends were ahead of me now. As I made my way back to the fellas, I looked at them and perceived that they had been watching - every heartbeat.

I walked away after they had finally stopped drilling me. I aimed for the sidewalk. Unfortunately, I had to pass the house known for the many dogs that would run out to the fence, biting, barking, and growling all at the same time. I really didn't like the way they were portraying themselves; you know - as if the fence wasn't there. I was relieved that I was making it into my house just before getting them roused.

Now that evening, I was within two houses before I had finally caught up with the waiting team. I noticed how they spoke to each other in low cryptic tones. I felt that maybe I should keep what was said strictly for me to myself because, by the way they stood silent as I approached them, I knew they expected some sort of information. However, I kept quiet as to see the envy and the jealousy eventually shift into the light amongst my so-called partners. Knowing that Alicia was in the air, I beckoned them on to aggravation.

"Hey, y'all just go on. I'll catch up later on tomorrow or something. See you at school. Y'all know we got a program too," I said lastly while walking away knowing in my mind that they could see me from the back of my head to my feet. I was pure angry red.

They caught up with me after a few seconds. I really didn't feel up to interrogation. So my attitude along the way was silent and non-attentive. There were many clouds in the sky and the day was giving way to nightfall. The bike, that I once had, would have gotten me away from this madness with one or two paddles, I thought remorsefully. But reality was none of such, for even now, the sounds of plotting were well in the making.

Their voices were now right at the back part of my head. This was not the conversation that had hints of goodness. I could not sense it at all.

"Hey, wait up a sec..."

Yeah, I had heard them clear enough but something inside just wasn't ready to submit anything to those goons.

"Hey, wus up? Ya gonna tell us what

happened back there or what?" they asked me.

"Well." I said after another several steps and then a complete stop. "I just asked her what's her name and all. That's pretty much it. The other two spoke up for her. I really don't think she even had time to respond."

"Ah dog...you so dumb," they said to me as they gave each other fives about it. Now this time I felt it was appropriate that the whole thing got a good shift into light. Only because of the fact that since I'd been there the attitudes went from cheery to aggravation. Whatever it may have been that I possessed, it was surely doing its job, for at that point, after those last spoken words, all reality ceased, and only anger remained in its place.

"I'm sick of y'all two constantly on me about who and what I choose to say. Man, wus-up with any one of you?" I responded back for them to evaluate a second or two.

They looked at each other and were like almost glad, as if they were ready and willing to fight it out. The first one ran up, swinging with more energy than there was power. After he threw a few selected misses, he caught me with a few. Then after a slight change in footing, I had the better swing. Not even two seconds had past before the other made his attack as well. He swung a couple of times before putting in a hit. Then there was a miss. Like the one before him, he was subdued as well. They did not know but I had been boxing far longer than they appear to have known.

The scene of the brawl ended with us going separate ways, trading glances of revenge, "to be prepared for the morrow" type of relationship.

I thought over our little scuffle on the way back to my house, about the different things - boys and women – men and girls - love and hate – now-n- laters - to the very Nikes and Addidas that covered our feet. Lastly, before entering the driveway, I thought it best to go ahead and put my clothes out for the next day. It was the honor roll program.

There wasn't going to be much time for me to get dressed now. I had awakened a little late this morning. Plus I had to iron my white church shirt, find my tie, and then do the impossible task of finding two dress shocks.

Now I was telling myself that if I were too late, I wouldn't be able to get in on who's sitting by whom. I would miss this little piece of boyhood interaction to our now approaching semi-physical type of relationship with the girls we had grown to know during the last five years. The situation for me was just that crucial.

It was going on 7:20 A.M. School started at 7:00 A.M. I felt nervous and shook by the announcement that maybe it would be best to wait just until getting to school, before I put on my best clothes. That wasn't what I wanted for such an occasion. It was supposed to be me up today, bright and early, dressed, and shinning. Then I was supposed to have been ready to be there amongst the quote unquote "elite of the class".

Over the intercom, they would announce for sixth graders' dismissal in order for us to go to the predestined seats. All of the cafeteria tables were long, with long metal benches along the bottom. These tables would fill up from the first ones being for the kindergarten all the way back. Grade by grade, they would gather until at last the whole place was packed.

All of us were feeling good, looking good, and loving it. The whole school would be seated in front of us as we stood one by one, waiting for each name to be called and for each student to walk across the stage. Yeah it was our little shines and periods of celebration that day.

I made it there just in time. Everything felt in place and perfect amidst the dozens of small ecstatic voices of my classmates. How intense these things were for us. Amazing I thought.

There wasn't anything like it. Yet, inside there also was a pit of shade and darkness. It was getting hard for me to ignore the sensations to just not do things like those that are expected. I told myself that during summer vacation days "I ain't doing nothing like books." I'm gonna just forget about school for a while and just reeee-laxx!

CHAPTER 4:
THE PARTY

Let the good days begin. It was now the end of May, and all of us began to realize this too. The hearts inside each of us were warm with the remembrance of each other. Every one that was seen, looked at, or touched was like the complete elementary bracket, and each individual was amplified through the minds. There were inspiring times as well as the trivial.

"Man y'all," a girl said, "we need to have a party or something.'

We all liked that idea instantly. It was a handshake and smile. City could have run for President after such a well-suggested plan. So each of us on the following day would bring something for the party. This was it. That included all of us, the whole boat, and the solid mix. This day we would see who wanted who for the last time as this group transformed into our 13th year of age.

The song on the radio today said something about "That's his girl now." I liked the song personally. I would rightly dedicate it to my choice among our little sweethearts. It was going to be a shocker and a time of rejoicing.

Learning the hard way was the only way that I seemed to learn. With every piece of information available, with all of the advice and corrective criticism, you'd think that a person could get the picture. You'd think that the message was comprehensive. No, not by me.

I got home from school today in full excitement about the fact that this was the last few hours of our childhood years, and to top it off, this would be the first party that we really would ever throw. The first thing on my "to do" list upon getting to the crib would be to contact my first Cuz and some ideal friends, just to pre-examine the upcoming fiesta. With the phone in hand and the numbers dialed, I waited. As if he were expecting a call my older cousin answered the phone.

"Cuz, what ya going to wear tomorrow?" I asked him.

"I might uh...I might wear my jeans with the t-shirt cause it's going to be live man. I want to be able to move around ya know? Maybe I'll walk up on lil' Kara and be like, "Hey, uh, how bout you and me?"

He asked me the same question and I agreed to wear pretty much the same outfit for the idea could compliment both our actions.

Thinking over my latest shirt and shorts combination was not easy. My legs had too many scars on them, so the selection was not the shorts. I felt that I also thought of my kaki pants. Those were pretty much for church. Initially then, the agreement was that we'd both be sporting a t-shirt and jeans outfit tomorrow. It had been a long and hard-fought battle with the dresser and closet. I had almost given my best to keep a little fashion into my attire.

Thinking to myself though, that next year it'll go down in the hallways and lunchroom. It'll go down during the programs and dances, all year. The one and only junior high prom would be preparing us for the all too famous high school prom.

"I'm through Cuz. See ya in the morning though. We'll just meet up extra early."

After the conversation ended, I sat back in full intake of the feeling one would have near Christmas, or birthdays. It was most definitely fresh ink. The urge to go to sleep now was upon me - waiting anxiously for the day ahead.

Immediately my next mission was to rummage around about my room until I had the perfect selection. It was going on 7:00 P.M.

"Okay Lenell, you can't let yourself

down tomorrow. When you see her, just remain your regular old self - no flexing, no intimidation, just your old, somewhat quiet, and slightly comical personality. It'll be a piece of cake!" I thought, while I laid my black jeans across the bed.

Then spotting a stack of folded shirts on the dresser, I screamed, "Piece of cake? Oh snap. I had forgotten that the store was to be one on the list. If I couldn't get to the store. I'd have to figure some other way to compensate. Now this was not a part of the plan, but now there was no more time for hesitation.

I had 7 dollars to my name so I was cool. However, I really hadn't planned to spend my last on anyone other than myself. But the thought of embarrassment and criticism ahead made me realize that it was better to donate to the cause instead of racking up points of disappointment and shock to the class.

"Yeah man, it is indeed going to be worth it - slicing the first slices for all of my little crushes."

The first person I saw was Michael. The other people he was talking to, I couldn't really see. I swallowed to gather nerves. So, down the hallway my walk was in motion. The entrance into the class was dead ahead. As I got closer, I could hear the outbursts and squeals of excitement. I could hear the walking, the noises of moving chairs, maybe the fondling of a bag of items. It was pure tension and joy.

"Lenell, wus-up? Hurry up man!"

"You can help us with the rest of the tables real quick!" Michael said to me. Now my pace livened a bit more. There was no more of the cool "intro" walk through the school's entrance doors. This was getting serious.

"See, the principal cooperated with us. They were calling the teacher to the office for a little while. We don't have too much time, really. It's about to go down up in here!" Michael was gleefully explaining to the passers, and yet on y to the few who were closest.

As I peered around the room, I could see all of our friends. All of us were preparing things along the tables. It was cookies ahoy ... drinks of all sorts...cups, plates, the worst and best of potato chips, and even a custom Nineteen Eighty-Eight radio and cassette player.

"Man," I thought, "this has to be a glimpse of the good days ahead."

That partner of mine and I made our way out into the hallway, keeping in mind to be cautious at every turn, fearing that the teacher could catch us! Therefore, at each door, we jumped and peaked through the small windows of the heavy school door. We were seeing that on each occasion it was clear to proceed.

The only sounds we made were our steps. The hearts within us beat loudly. I thought for a slick second my homeboy could hear it. Also with an odd noise, came horseplay. By the time we made it to the office section of the main building, with the same precautious measures of course, we spotted that good teacher of ours just as she was about to leave the office.

I turned to run. He turned as well ... tit ... for ...tat. We were at it - back to the confines of the classroom with seconds at stake. We burst through those doors like forty going north, full speed ahead. The lockers on each side of me flew by like lightning!

As our teacher walked into the room, she suddenly hesitated, looked at us, and said, "y'all threw this party for yourselves. This is not a party for me."

We had no room to argue the point that she saw fit to convey. We were more like, if it was indeed the truth; then let the truth free us to go on along with the party. Therefore, after a few more words she gave us permission to start the party.

The music resumed and the atmosphere quickly became as the moments before. I couldn't help but notice how the girls no longer seemed like playmates. I felt myself wanting to touch hands, even wanting to kiss one of them. Not knowing where to begin, it was better that I lay low and maybe in the process, learn a thing or two.

The time for us to drink and eat had arrived. The music was perfect now so in instances you could see sort of couple like situations forming about. You could see small talk and the looks of concern across the faces.

There on the farther side of the room I could see one of my homeboys "lil' Mike." He seemed to be adjusting quite nicely, I thought enviously. I wondered about the things of which they possibly could have been talking so attentively. Everyone seemed to be in couples. Then, an inside voice alerted me to the status. There was no more rehearsal time. It was show time for sure!

I had to study something as simple as walking. I was so nervous. Walking to that table would be the most calculated walk of steps I think that I had ever made. There was no room to trip, drag, or bump my converse on anything. I was destined to keep the soda off my freshly ironed jeans. By all means, chocolate was to be no-where near my bright, fresh, straight-out-of-the washer t-shirt, with the open button-down over-shirt.

The only thing in between me and the one I figured this day would be best was my not too friendly classmate, "Brenda", the one who had sat directly in front of me. She and I had gone sour due to a former beginning of the school year desk-to-desk confrontational issue. It was about my feet being on the bottom back of her desk. Maybe I did disrupt a few hundred of her daydream escapades, but in no way could I let that interfere with such a delightful engagement.

"Hey, wus up Bren? Are we going to get cool now since there ain't any more of my over-active tennis shoes and me? Anyway though, what school y'all going to next year?" I asked the all of the girls. I wisely spoke. "Y'all' was the key word, the link that I needed to extend to her other conversation perhaps!

Brenda spoke words, but each one went right past my ears into the air and breath of the other students. I think she laughed or made a joke of some kind. I didn't even notice. The only thing I awaited was the sweet response of Alicia, and it had to be obvious as I stood there soaking my eyes into hers. Flashes of trees and hidden dark places crept Into mind. All of a sudden, I had feelings to tint the lights. I wanted romance in the air 100%.

She said to me, "You gonna keep drawing and stuff? You be drawing some cool pictures." I heard her perfectly. The sounds around us must have ceased, with hers amplified to the max, in slow motion, but with no trace of the lagging sound.

"Always," I said to her thankfully.

"It ain't too much else that I'm good at other than running through woods and stuff. I do that a lot, I guess." I couldn't believe what came out of my mouth. Here I was giving her the image of me with the Tarzan outfit, lions, tigers, and bears. Oh my.

"That's cool though y'all gone do what y'all do. But you think you could draw me a picture right fast?" Alicia asked.

I simply thought to myself, "Pencil and paper, don't fail me."

"I ain't that good at portraits, and as much as I would like to draw a picture of you, I really don't think it would be good enough. I really don't think that it would be like it's supposed to be."

She gestured for me to take a seat along side of hers, so I did. I walked over to where it was that she sat, only not even four seconds later, to take a seat upon someone else's leftovers.

"I'll be back," I said to her.

The expression I had while looking at the mess on my clothes would make one think for a second that I had never seen anything like it before in life. In all honesty, it was no more than a little cake, maybe a smudge of chocolate. However, the embarrassments made me over exaggerate the problem.

So away, I walked into the land of lost cool points. I think I was down to like a negative 10, after that altercation. Feeling more at ease once I got out of direct sight, a sigh of shame escaped my grasp. It echoed off the walls of our golden stroll hallway. Maybe upon my return I'd give the old art skills a chance, anything to re-enact the vibe we had going before my unawareness caused such a devastating chain of events.

While in the restroom, I remembered the many battles fought in such a small place. Yeah this was finally the end of elementary, and the next phase, being teenagers with dates and the like. Not as much brawling would happen, but instead just the opposite. Rushing to finish my task, hastily I got on back down to the party.

Isn't that just like a pirate, entering the class? I could already see yet another dude in the very place where I was supposed to be. He wasn't around us earlier, but still, it looked as if she were indeed enjoying the company! I felt betrayed, but still I pulled what was left of my cool type suit of armor together, and reintroduced myself.

My armor fell one piece at a time, after seeing what I had seen. This person even had the nerve to touch on her hair, as pretty as it was. This pretty much did the most damage. I decided to be merely the fourth wheel in the conversation.

"Hey, what's up Kev?" I rolled out the side of my mouth.

"Nothin' man, just keeping the girls entertained and thangs."

As I looked at him smile with confidence, my eyes felt as if they were turning into burning coals. This was beginning to feel like maybe the scene whereby a discrepancy could be aroused!

"Hey dude, let me holler at 'er for a second. Give us some space right fast," I said.

"What you mean?" she shot back at me. "He can stay with us. We ain't together. So why not?" Alicia said.

I knew then that my world and hers weren't on the level that I hoped that they could be. "I, uh, may be back y'all. Let me see wus up with everybody," I said as I narrowed down the list in my mind. While I thought about it, there really weren't too many at all on my list. A slight gloom settled over me. I told myself quietly that I'd just be better off with the punch and cookies.

Then things changed, upon hearing a voice. "Hey Lenell, you ain't gonna kick it with me none? What's up?" Linda said to me.

She was kind of cute and all, I might add. It just could work out!

How many times had I looked at her during the years and not noticed her acute interest in my being. There were many times now that I think about it, that we did share some close encounters. The field trip, the science project, and whilst in the music room, are just a few occasions. I do remember the way she slick-listened as we missed on a note or two, but still she revealed no signs of fatigue.

So, what was it that kept me just from appreciating the real value of such a welcoming friend? I wondered. In some ways, she rather reminded me of myself. She wasn't the best dresser. She wasn't as popular as the other girls. I guess she pretty much kept everything somewhat low-key, which was another behind-the-scenes motivator.

"Hey look, you know it's a chance that

most of us will probably lose contact after this." She seemed to agree while she got noticeably closer. I felt an urge to relax. I was actually feeling somewhat comfortable in this newly sprung world of passion!

"Ah ... ya wanna talk sometimes after this? ... Maybe keep contact? You know, we are sort of like good friends," she said while taking the pen from my shirt pocket in order to write down her telephone number. I looked ahead into what I saw as a good future, replying, "It's all good."

CHAPTER 5:
THE NEW NEIGHBORHOOD

School was out now for the summer vacation. I had no idea of what I was to do next. It all became much clearer to me after hearing the news of us moving. Now was the short time to tell all my partners around the hood that it was all good and saying goodbyes to the luscious fruit trees.

Still though, the newly found ground was still an inspiration to me. What would the people be like? Would there be many girls in the neighborhood? What junior high school would we attend?

It wasn't fun carrying the many boxes to the truck. It wasn't fun watching my old friends get smaller in the back window. They threw the peace sign. It wasn't going to be fun unloading all the stuff that we were destined to unload.

My birthday was coming so I was really in a "hurry up and get situated" kind of anxiety. After a fifteen-minute drive, we pulled up along side this nicely shaped brick house, with a good-sized lawn that went uphill. That meant for sure that my brother and I would be out there many summers to come, as sure as the sun sets. We all got out of the vehicle and walked up the incline of the driveway - each of us from all ages, interested.

It took us a couple of days to get the house organized, but we did it rather impressively. Our room was in the front of the house, whereby out the window, you could see the front yard.

There were other houses directly across the street. There also was the combined junior high and high school. A curious smile spread across my face - one that showed devious intuition. Would the proximity of the school help or hurt me I wondered?

Today was a bright and clear day. Nervousness about stepping outside to examine the area was upon me now that it was daylight. From our yard, one could see a few fellows about my age, and some older ones talking amongst themselves.

"Don't trip man!" I told myself.

Besides, we were the (quote un quote) new family on the block! So perceiving it was the normal way of things. I cast my gazes along other hidden valleys as well. All the same, it was time to get familiar with this new neighborhood. My brother came out the door a minute or two later. We both were anxious to travel the unknown land. We decided to play catch in the front yard where the others could see. They not only saw us, but began to walk in our direction. There were two of them.

One was somewhat tall. The other was on the heavier side. My internal soldier instinct activated, as we perceived that they intended to meet us. My brother went back into the house only to return with two boxing gloves, thus making me to wonder which of the two boys I would eventually box.

"What's y'all name?" the taller one asked. After learning each other's names, they rather hipped us to what the street was like.

"Y'all wanna box a little?" my brother asked them. Unknown looks of concern trickled across our expressions for we all knew that even though it would be fun and games, still the fact of the matter would be one losing, and the other victorious!

"We got one glove a piece," my brother said. He handed one glove to me. It was the left glove even though I was right handed. He gave the other one to the fellow known as "Shannon." I wondered about the possibility of me put to shame so soon, and by no chance could I start the area with a reputation of weakness.

Yet, after the signal, we let off immediately into the punch out! I guess my former neighborhood had prepared me for this all too familiar affair. I don't recall being hit. It was over so soon. The outcome was also the same as I can remember just not with as close as much sweat and skill necessary. Most of my punches were accurate enough though. We learned that this was a hell of a way to introduce one's self. Yet it was the only true introduction. Maybe it was best that we understood each other, to avoid any disrespect.

My brother then began the next match with the taller of the two. He also was the winner and presumed that the word would spread around. Yeah, the two new boys would most definitely make some enemies, and maybe some curious girlfriends that were peeking here, and over yonder!

The next day we would be going South for a few days. I rather liked this because by golly, we had all kinds of motor vehicles to drive. We even had access to the very family car itself! There were the different livestock, such as roosters, chickens, chicks, hogs, and damn near the works. We even became accustomed to firearms such as rifles and handguns together!

The first day we had a three-wheeler to ride. We got good at some of the small stunts until at one time; I almost lost my head -

courtesy of an unseen clothesline. As I sat on the machine however, and prepared the gear for first, my cousin hopped on the back along with me. After releasing the brakes, I looked down at the surrounding area yet all the time moving forward. As my head began to search up for travel, the line caught my throat, pulling the wheel off the ground, tilting the wheel up, and off the ground!

The three-wheeler kept going for a couple or more feet. Once the wheel finally hit the ground, there was a distant sound of laughter, from different areas, as I lay there, on my back against the semi-wet mud.

My hands went immediately about my neck, touching searchingly for some sign of blood! It was intense and horrific! I could have sworn that someone cut my throat wide open!

I was too scared to look at my hands. The laughs discontinued, and turned more into panic chatter. I laid there for a minute or so thanking the good Lord that my neck hadn't slit. All the same, I swore vengeance on that machine.

The next evening after I had recovered some from the pain, there was a water puddle nearby. We had access to the keys, so it was up to us if we wanted to ride or not. We only had to be careful about the gas and injury side of the coin.

And there it was, parked near the tree in the back part of the house, still looking as if it was laughing from the other day. I managed to get it started after a minute or two of tugging the cord.

Once ignited, I headed straight for the cotton field. I needed power for stunting, and not speed. So around and around I tore into the soft hills of the field, breaking apart the parallel strips of earth!

Further down the muddy road that the tractors used in their goings and comings, I spotted an even more suitable water spot for me to plunder, making that my next destination! It only took me twenty seconds to get there. Upon entering the water, there was a sudden, very large wave of water thrown into the air! I resembled a tornado with all of the debris and muddy waters slung about!

After a few more minutes of this, I grew tired. So off to the house I coasted, watching the cotton rows pass, a section at a time. I listened to the engine's sound as I sped up and eased off the throttle. After making it to the porch, I saw that my brother and cousin were about to drive to the store, so I happily decided to trail them. They got into the car so I restarted the engine. We rode on out onto the dirt road and on toward the street.

"Hey y'all don't drive too fast," I yelled to them as we now were close to the on-coming pavement.

As the car took off, I was right behind them, giving the machine the throttle that it needed to keep up. But as it was time to change into a higher gear, it didn't. I then noticed that it wasn't gaining any more speed as well. Our pops was watching from the front porch and I think he heard the strange noise, now coming from the engine. My heart was feeling the sort of feeling you would get after breaking one of the more valuable toys.

When I had finally made it back to the yard for parking and examination, Dad said, "The transmission has burned out." That happens by not charging the gears out of first. It could have happened during my mud-splashing escapade in that all too famous water puddle!

I sat there on the porch and waited patiently for my brother and cousin to return. How did I manage to destroy our three-wheeler? Sometimes, it just felt like I couldn't keep anything long enough to enjoy.

The robots that we got for Christmas, I broke the head on mine. What's a toy robot without a head? The battery-operated machine gun, the piece that held the batteries in place broke. I ran my battery-operated car through a puddle of water, and it died out on me. The funny thing is, that's probably what I'm going to need to tell my brother that I ran it through some water.

They rolled up after a few more minutes. I stood to walk out. Might as well get it over with I assumed.

"Hey, the three-wheeler don't even change gears no more," he said and looked at me. I was feeling the aggravation that I had caused. I felt sorry. A few more minutes passed and I found that we really weren't fazed by the loss.

We were natural fun-raisers from the head to the toe, thoroughbred action conjurers of exciting times!

"Y'all wanna have target practice?" my cousin asked us. We began to look around for targets.

I wasn't the best shot, and I felt jealous of my older brother and cousin. They seemed to hit most of their targets, while I hit the dirt it seems as on both sides of the object and exposing the dirt that would arise out of gunfire. I was embarrassed so to speak. I couldn't even shoot straight, and that bothered me.

We went on continuing to set up everything that we could use for a target: gin bottles, beer bottles, beer cans, soda cans. Everything had a small .22 bullet hole in one place or the other.

Finally after waiting patiently for them to lose interest, they eventually did. This allowed me full access to the rifle for the dispersal of all the remaining ammunition and I felt like hunting "Wabbits".

In Mississippi, you were in a world of your own. Couldn't too many other people deal with the mosquitoes and spray cans, the crickets, bees, the wasps, the frogs, the snakes, hawks, raccoons, squirrels, rabbits, coyotes, bulls, cows, the pigs and hogs, chickens, roosters, the summertime heat, and the winter-wood chopping, other than us. Down South was always a nice get away. I don't want to be misunderstood; it wasn't for the weak of heart.

Our neighborhood was still new to us too. We had barely explored the street itself in completion. Man were we wasting time, for it was the very end of June. All of our eyes and ears were tuned in on our parents. We were listening to the facts of the upcoming "Fourth of July".

They noticed us rummaging around, with enquiring minds. Fireworks were the days of our youth! We expected to be participants in the Roman candle wars, and the bottle rocket stampedes!

"Let's ask if we are going to get some fireworks today."

That was the question to ask by my little sister, my brother, and me. The oldest of us was my sister, Kayly. She was kind of out of the fireworks stage, which meant more for us. After seeing what appeared to be preparations to leave, we all sat quietly for we didn't want to disturb the tempo. We were extremely close to what we wanted. Not wanting to appear over anxious was the idea but once we got outside, it was hard to hide the feelings engulfing us.

Once in the car, I sat in my seat and began to strategize my tactics of warfare. "Ya think everyone's going to meet over here?" I asked Randy.

"Nope all us going over grandma's house."

This wasn't too bad, since we had moved to a new neighborhood anyway. They probably couldn't handle our type of deal, I told myself strictly for comforts sake. But still, I wanted to be there to see for myself.

After returning, we instantly grabbed the bags to look through the dandy selection of ammunition. It would be a good, long battle. We had dozens of rockets, and Roman candles for tomorrow night's shindig!

The weatherman's forecast stated, "Scattered showers for tomorrow." But the sky was so clear. Yet and still, there was a kind of breeziness about the wind. The smell of moisture wasn't evident in the air, so this calmed me just enough to relax. By then it was 7:15 in the evening. Every so often, you could spot one of the large puffy clouds seemingly very far away to affect such a welcomed holiday. Still the so-called weatherman had spoken.

"Looks like the clouds are over Arkansas and Mississippi," I thought.

If I could have walked farther, everyone would see me walking the city searching for evidence of tomorrow's forecast. Panicking, I thought, "It couldn't rain on the 4th."

We all had our newest shoes and shorts, the fresh new shirts as well (man-uh plea-se!). Wanting to free my mind from the worry of approaching catastrophe, I asked my brother, "Hey, Rand! what we goin' do if it rains tomorrow?"

He was into one of the movies that had just come on TV. That cable really had most of his attention but still he answered. "We just uh pop 'em the night after."

But I myself was feeling like man, I want sunshine to the night, the food, the Bar-b-cue aromas, and people running and hopping about, and kinfolks playing cards! Things were most definitely going to be a tad unsupervised, thus for enabling me for perhaps an undetected beer.

Everybody was up early today. There were bags of charcoal to get. There we were with grills to be set up. There was trash about to be collected and an all-too-famous bush hedging needed all the way down the lawn.

"Y'all gone out there and fill the tank with gas. Check the oil in it before you try cranking it," Pops told us.

So after finishing our breakfast, we sat there and zoned out on the last minutes of some karate movie. We were being slick trying to see which of us would start cutting first.

There always was a situation of who would cut the front or backyard. My brother liked those karate movies; so I decided to start on the front first, to relieve him of not having to miss the end of the movie. It was a little smaller than the backyard. The backyard had rocks hidden in the grass, and the roots were unseen under the crab grass of which was most of it, thus making the blade to clank on contact with the hidden wood.

The front yard on the other hand, had the neighbors' daughters walking the different yards. Sometime they were on bikes, while others took the dogs out for a walk.

The band practiced every other day out on the blacktop near the school. This scene was beginning to set on me quite nicely. This new street was alright so far, I suspected.

The task appeared to be simple, but that was not the case for me. I kept slipping up behind the lawnmower on the spots where the grass was taller and thicker. I even wanted a riding lawnmower at one time, but never would anything like that escape from my mouth.

It wasn't too bad though, for today was the fourth of July. Everything about us was going to work out for the best today. For as soon as we were finished with our chores, then would be the dress up!

I wondered who would be there for me to impress! Everyone there would be family, not real girlllllssss! These thoughts sent jitters down my spine. I cut the lawnmower off to observe the yard for either satisfaction or touch up.

"Hey I'm finished cutting the front," I said to my parents as I stood there examining the debris clinging to my shirt and pants, hoping that I could possibly hold a few one-dollar bills, but being extra cautious not to push. I entered my room and glanced at the clothes and fireworks that packed the bag.

"It's about to be war," I whispered, with a smile coming to my face, while looking at the clear evening day.

My brother could use the car occasionally now that he was sixteen, and this was no way to get bored. This meant mobilization. This meant the group of us cruising around looking for the hippest scenery. This meant that we could slip away from the parental eyes, and escape into a world of action and adventurous scheming right after we returned from the cookout. I was most definitely planning to keep clean. There was no telling where we might ride, such as by the mall, to the parks, and in our old neighborhood perhaps.

"Go ahead and grab the firecrackers and throw 'em in the car so we won't forget 'em," Bro said to me.

With no hesitation, I went off to accomplish the task before me. With both bags in hand, my peripheral vision could distinguish that extremely large package of roman candles. It looked as if we would get at least ten a piece.

Incense was not going to cut it this time. We had a fresh pack of lighters because there was no time to lose accuracy and suffer hits, by not being able to light the fuse appropriately. Now everyone was dressed and prepared to leave. Mom and Pop, and our sisters all rode off together ahead of us, whilst that brother of mine and two of my cousins jumped into the car and sat back with laughter and excitement, talking over our list of undecided adventure!

My older cousin was splitting a cigar and I wondered why he did it. He told me, "It's called rolling a blunt!" What happened to the small, white sheets was a mystery to me.

CHAPTER 6:
THE 4TH OF JULY

We might have to make a detour or two. I was considering the radiant spirit within each of us as we sat in those seats on the car cruise. The car, with a decent bag of thunder, was now very, very, hyped up!

Being a true stranger to that much indulgence was an extra 4th's celebration for me. While on the roll, we eventually pulled up along side of a vaguely familiar face. Hoping to get the info as into what this area would be like after sunset, my brother got out of the car first, then my cousin Reece as well.

Key and I just remained in the backseat, with the reminder of the cigar to ourselves. As we smoked, we could hear them talking amongst themselves.

"Hey, y'all having a war tonight?" my brother asked the guy who we soon would come to know as Seal.

He told us about the different streets that would load up their works. People would be walking the block in search of anyone else that was interested in such a dangerous way to play! We were all excited about it so we decided to go back a little later, right after we feasted on our famous bar-b-cue cookouts.

By the time we pulled up, everyone was "crunk" so to speak. My uncles were all in the atmosphere of crowds from here to there instantly, spreading curse words and laughter about, crushing beer cans, ever on the lookout for the next case!

My aunties were rampant with the food preparations and of course, the gentle tug of maybe the newest member of our family about their legs. The pre-teens and mostly all of us had some form of fireworks, so the adults were always yelling for one of us to take the firecrackers to a distant place, plus sharing a few cursing words!

We all got out of the car and began to expand to the horizon, of excitement and civilized chaos! We made our way to the head of the household, the grandparents. We hugged and greeted our grandparents. Afterwards the hectic ness let loose on the family grounds. It was everyman for himself.

We spoke and quickly grabbed a younger child or two that were the younger fellows in the family of cousins, enabling ourselves to perform the latest karate or wrestling technique on 'em. It was only natural for them to bear some of the brutalities that our older uncles had performed on us as young children. Our motto was punishment is fun when you just happen to be a boy amongst the family.

"Hey let's go eat 'cause it's getting kind of dark," my brother conveyed to the crew, as we were sitting in the company of all or most of my grandmothers' children, with newly glistened eyes which gave the signals of highness to the suspecting older generation.

"Hey y'all, I'm uh going outside. Hold my plate for me," my cousin said to me, leaving me all of a sudden with an empty dish of remnants upon my lap. We were all excited and it was showing. We gathered in the back of the house, where the men sat about in chairs, close to the grill with the blues blaring on the radio! The scene was subtle enough for the actual (if a teen got a beer) "they didn't sweat cha'" kind of atmosphere. We sat around, cigarettes burning, cigars lit, and half-empty gin bottles posted on the card table. What an evening I felt after my second beer.

"Aye let me grab the bag out the car," I said to my brother. Little did I know he had already decided that this was now the time for us to leave.

"Gather up the troops," I said to myself with the glaze of fire inside my eyes.

Sooooo.... after about 3 or 4 more face grabs, plus chops on our unsuspecting pre-teen cousins, I made it out the back to spot De-che, my younger cousin. Yes, he was younger than I was, and after him Termile, then was me. Over us were ReCee, then my brother and him with a set of car keys. Plus we had a bag of rockets, flares, and with the bonus of new territory to rampage!

"Hey y'all, let's roll out," I yelled, and they looked and heard me. They threw their cans away and exchanged the summing up of the views amongst my drunken yet directing and slash punishing, slash party starting, slash street running uncles.

As they got closer, I kept in mind to brace myself, because we were all good for catching each other off guard with pranks. It never ended, and that was all good. We finally got out onto the front porch to say our goodbyes. After enough spoken words, off to the car we walked.

After hearing each door open for a second, then close 4 times, it meant we all were properly seated. But alas, fire with thrill and the passion of the night was calling us! Therefore, my brother started the car.

With bar-b-cue sauce fresh on my fingertips, I had already given my new lighter, "sure not to fail me", fuse igniter a few strikes for a test drive.

"Hey man stop striking that lighter. It's blowing my high," Cuz yelled back to me from the front seat.

The tape we were listening to was a local group. They spoke of clothes and cars. They spoke of money and women, with each track seemingly more interesting than the last. "How could I live like that?" I wondered.

I saw a couple people on their stroll on our way down the street where we were cruising. At the same time I was extending my hand to receive the newly rolled blunt, still fresh with the moisture of the roller's crafty work. Then it moved silently to the left of me to my younger cousin, after a few seconds or so.

My whole soul was blazing with what seemed like my last great 4th of July celebration. The night had finally set down on us. There was no longer the anxiousness of arrival, by fact that this was the time indeed. We got back to our new hood. We got out of the car! Everyone out there was ready for war!

You would have needed some eye protectors, maybe even long sleeve shirts. We had neither. Anyone on the side watching, would see the debris and fire trails to explosions, smoke streams to your every direction, directly beside you or right above your head if not in direct contact. All of this meant that you were targets, and they were the targets.

Once we were ten minutes into our bag of fireworks, a full fledge battle had arisen. There was no parlay, or exchange of battle talk, only fuses and hot lighters! I needed focus to concentrate on the moving obstacles.

The roman candles were the most selected. So it was pure danger to be under direct fire. They would quickly zoom off into the selected crowd causing panic and confusion.

I lost all sense of caution and lit the fuses with speed. "Let's take it closer. We got 'em backing up some," I was yelling, smiling, and taking cover at the same time. We all were. This probably was our greatest and therefore one of the last true forth of July celebrations. We would make it count!

CHAPTER 7:
THE GIRL NEXT DOOR

"Hey, can I wear ya Raiders T-shirt?" I asked my brother the next morning. This was the day after the Fourth of July celebration had finally passed. He just opened his eyes and closed them, with the nod and the turn of a head direction.

I had made close ties with the street now, and it was making it easier to conversate. Out on the porch there were firecracker remnants, sticks, and box flares burned to a crisp! The street was the scene of something major. It was all a memory now, I was thinking; and a good one indeed!

It was somewhat hot this morning and the sky was bright, with the sun blazing. "It's probably too early right now," I said to the houses that lined the sidewalk and street, the mailboxes, and the light poles. I was thinking about everyone who may have been inside them, either still asleep, or dreaming, or up into the television.

My mom looked out of the front door as I stood outside, giving me the O-K for the clean up. I looked around at the scene thinking, "Oh, what a night!"

With every piece of used firework, I tried to remember the event as it was. With some of the more popular fireworks I picked up, I could revive a couple of details, a brief take back to the live smoke and fire. My hands had received quite a few burns due to bottle rockets and the flare fire of the Roman candles. It was to me the most favorable 4th.

Inside I knew that it would only fade from now. I felt that since we were at this age, most of these holidays would now be passed along to the next generation. We had so many memories of the former holidays as well, so, time was due to change us over into the witnesses of the whole other aspect of life and loving becoming teenagers on into adults.

In all, it took me over an hour to clean the area of our property, and I was somewhat thankful for it. I now could say that the faces next door were now becoming the sharers of our generational development. The fun ahead and the drama were all dawning in on me like mist or dew.

"Man, I would of let you know, if I knew.

But how could I tell you when I hadn't even heard about it myself?" I heard voice express out. By the tone of the speaker's voice, I could tell that he may have been on a defensive position of some situation.

"Man, you could have called me and let me know she was over there. Y'all just didn't seem to want me around or some'n punk!" the other fellow said in return.

From just these few years of life I became very transitive (so to speak) of another's vibe. This one was an all-too-familiar sight - the partner fall out over maybe, a sudden new girl on the scene. I felt the other's pain and instantly began to share the spirit of disapproval.

"Yeah, just like the good 'ole days," I said silently, as I scanned the remaining area for further waste disposal, turning my attention off the two fellows and on into the path to the trash for the last drop. I wondered if this girl was worth all the drama.

I was feeling a rush. School would be starting soon enough!

"Man, oh boy!" I really began to like the new street of mine. It had everything a developing boy like me needed. There was the ultimate vitamin "A" which was "action". Across the street from us lived a family of six.

My younger sister would sometimes wonder across the street to their house to play with the younger girls of the family. I never really went over there, because the boys in their family were somewhat younger than me. Also, there was nothing good they could learn from me at their age.

Then one particular afternoon, I noticed something different - another presence at their house. As I was walking from a game in my hommie's driveway, I saw the man of the house removing suitcases from his car. There was a pink chest of some sort, and another smaller white suitcase. A car with extremely loud music passing by offered me a break in my train of thought though. Yet satisfied with today's street embrace, I re-entered the house, all the while hearing the music get lower and lower.

The moment my eyes opened, I could hear that a radio was playing, a radio outside our house. It could be the kid next door, washing his mother's car, I assumed, but then again, it wasn't gospel music, and that was the only music to which he tended to listen.

So once my eyes adjusted to the light of the day and I placed on my shorts and t-shirt. My second actions were toward the window of our junked up action-packed bedroom to spot our neighbor's latest visitor. She was a little high on the beauty scale, so I felt inside that in all maybe we could just speak once or twice, 'cause her relationship would probably get started with one of the more popular fellows on our block.

But man, I thought, she held the frame to the picture. She was tight! My inner connection of schemes began to tick. I felt that I needed some form of passion history to backup the fellows' talks, to and from school. Yes school was once again to begin in a few weeks. That would be the good old 7th grade year for me.

I felt awkward asking my little sister about the new person across the street. But in all honesty, I felt justified. The new girl did stay directly across the street from our house. In the mental handbook of a boy's life, that is rule #1 which states that "whoever is closest to you in your neighborhood, then she indeed will be within reach either slick romantically, or in the other which is the sister kind of connection."

Anyway, I was feeling like "Why I can't be the first to try at least with a friendly conversation?" The bouncing ball, with the laughter of competition caught my sight. The faces on the court were now familiar ones - my brother and his new friends. They were well into one of their famous games of "twenty-one".

Sensing that this was an opportunity for a stroll, yet slightly nervous, I hesitated before walking into the outside world. I knew in the back of my mind that I had slick intensions of waving at least at our new friend!

As I looked in the mirror, looking over my young smile, I figured that maybe I shouldn't show my teeth too much.

"Has anyone seen the remote control?" "Has anyone seen my car keys?" There was one voice, that of my mother's, and the other being our ever, Southbound, slash Chicago father. I did not like looking for either of the two items for them, so this was indeed my "out" cue. It was as if I were being pushed out of the house by my semi-laziness, plus determinations for a new friendship!

I quickly looked down the street and up the street, as if I were trying to catch a wave; a wave of action and a good day's lurking. Noticing the door open across the street made me realize that I couldn't just openly gaze into their door. That would be inappropriate.

But man, I sure intended on meeting the owner of that pink suitcase. I saw the opportunity of someone taking me into the confines of the two-story home that the family had occupied probably a while before we had even arrived on the street.

Unfortunately, at the most passionate times in my life, I always seem to be religious. I was always saying "Oh my God!" However this time, I cast lines of Shakespeare mixed with the paraphrased and complimented attributes of beauty, around her radiant person, off sight!

There wasn't any denial of my full hesitation on the porch. I stood still to internalize all of her actions. I wondered how I would get close enough to the street, knowing that I could fumble if I tried to speak and it ended up being awkward due to miss-timed waving. Then there would be unheard words.

But an idea struck me that could get my

young body into the angle I needed. To catch the proper introduction before my little, personality was overwhelmed by the other block -burners in our hood, I decided that I would empty the trash. That way I'd look good in both worlds. Almost desperate, I remembered that the trash could be emptied even if it really didn't need it. This was my passport to Loveland!

Since the days were still warm, I could be seen wearing a pair of shorts! As I grew, I felt better about the appearance of my legs. The marks and cuts from childhood had faded a little bit. To have finally accomplished true leg beauty, the two matching white socks made it easier to sport 'em. There were Reebok teenagers around, but I myself chose K-Swiss all-white, low top. In my hand was now the trash-bag passport.

Yeah, the all too famous visitor was outside sure enough, and I was in direct view, as I had hoped to be. I saw immediately down the street all of the now baby NBA drafts. I knew it was them because before attempting some fantastic shot, they would yell out their names. All of this was the Jordan's hoops and all the Magic Johnson's passes, let them tell it. The shots were never just from themselves who had made the shot.

Talking about a good wave of action to catch, this one would take me clean to the shores of my first kisses. Dare I say more? "Operate, ole man!" If this is pre-adult life, at what point did I lose my childhood?

I am now at least 400 miles from Memphis, Tennessee; I thought as the trembling of the Greyhound Bus alerted me constantly, depriving me of any lengthy daydreaming opportunity. My earphones alerted men that I was running low on battery power. So the tape that I kept flipping repeatedly began to drag a little bit.

Onward though, I headed to a new beginning in my mind. This would be on the mile high streets of Denver, Colorado. The territory was also the land of my youth, even before the all-famous Memphis, Tennessee. I had no idea how I'd make a dollar for myself, but then I reflected over my past in such a city as it was and as long as it was there, there was pretty much a self-sustaining consciousness about life. The city of Denver prepares one well to survive with bottom line basics!

I rocked a lot in my seat as I tried to calm myself down. My last few hours in the hood reflected most of my lifestyle while I was there - the liquor store runs, then on to the weed and at least a gram of white. It never occurred to me that I didn't handle sitting still well while so intoxicated and high, so I suffered for a long time during the first few hundred miles. I felt as if I were dying.

"Let us stop please, Lord, so I can smoke one cigarette." I prayed whilst looking out the tinted grayish bus window. In fact, I think the only thing that got me through this journey, was (God) of course, and a strange woman named Anna, who decided to sit beside me after seeing me in such a peculiar state.

"Hey, wus up!" She said with a smile.

I slowly responded, "I'm on my way to Colorado."

"Where ya headed?"

She was a little on the heavy side but it seemed to me that it never could have been a problem for her while coming up. That thought came to me from the simple fact of her vibes from the first words she spoke to me. The voice relaxed me an awful lot. I was now in a state wherein I felt conversation would be attainable, and boy was I in need of company. My unstableness was near a peak, but through constant trial and error I knew and could tell when I was over the peak and on the way down. Therefore I felt the sensations to relax.

She offered me cinnamon ginseng tablets. In fact she gave me two of them. It wasn't quite medicine, but in my situation, I would have tried anything. After consumption and a few minutes, the worst part of my anxiety was OVER.

CHAPTER 8:
THE LONG BUS RIDE

The seats in which we sat only leaned back so far, meaning you did nothing after the first 10 hours but fantasize about stretching out completely. Animosity actually crept into your mind. I dreamed of exchanging Anna for the passenger directly in front of me, or for the one behind as well. The seats double-teamed any chance of a person's positioning of comfort.

Slumped over is how I rested. Straight tiredness overwhelmed the struggle for exact comfort-ness. So slowly but surely, I fell into a slumber. As I began to awaken into the dawning of the next day, I noticed large boulders scattered about the area along the side of the highway.

One thing was certain. Denver is famous for its mountains and for its cleanliness. Then again, it still had the mile high streets! I needed to practice caution and a lot of speculation, for this city could bury you fast.

A feeling of completion was running through my soul like electric adrenaline! Suppressed anxiety, mixed with eagerness, had me up in the seat now looking for bigger and bigger land stones.

"We gotta be closer 'cause I'm damn near about to collapse," I said to the window beside my face. With each word, there was a piece of fog due to breath upon each exhale.

One of the highway signs signified that we only had a few hundred miles to go. Another smile of anticipation set across my face. "Man, man, man," I thought. "Boy, oh boy!"

Our bus pulled over at a rest stop 200 miles from town. There was a McDonald's there. So the routine would be that the smokers immediately posted up for a couple of smokes, while the children and other adults lined up for food. Choosing the latter, I walked off to myself spotting a clear bench not far from where we parked. I had a lot on my mind to sort out.

I was remembering that I just dropped and abandoned a life for the unknown adventure into which I propelled myself. Lighting a cigarette and observing the scenery was an all too welcoming sight for me. "Man," I thought, "I finally escaped the hood. It's cool though. It was long over due."

I thought a little longer. Flashbacks came of the history of my life, and the excellent mistakes. Then came the clean get-away after, the thousands of blunts that were rolled and burned under the music of Three-Six Mafia, Kingpin Skinny Pimp, Playa-Fly, Man, and the times them niggas got me thru.

I seemingly just up and left. "This better be for the good," I said while exhaling the smoke mixed with my words.

Sure enough, those few minutes of break arrived and passed. Sure enough, we mounted the bus again and continued on to the destination. Thank God! At this point, I really preferred to finish the trip on out – not anymore hesitations. Any more stops would absolutely destroy me, I felt.

But what was the big hurry? I found myself thinking. What was it that I longed for? How much different would my life actually be? True enough I was entering another state sort of on the west coast of the United States, but how much more different could it be from my original southern state?

Spanish was spoken fluently before and behind me, which let me know, at the moment, that there seemed to be a high quantity of Mexican persons on board the bus. It was clear that they weren't getting off on the previous city stops. Were all headed for the same area? Did I miss an exit? Am I headed to Mexico?

I wondered, "Is this the same city I left as a youngster? Are there any familiar people left in this state of my youth?" I was puzzled. I was confused. But also, I was anxious sure enough!

"Getting it on" by Playa Fly had me up and lively in my seat now, after this 36-hour trip. The lights of the bus station at night lit me up! I was ready to do the damn thing for whatever it might be. It seemed like the passengers in front of me just weren't moving fast enough. They all waited 'til it was exiting time exactly before they reached up to grab which and whatever items they had rescued from the abodes of their former state.

With my focus straight outside our windows, I saw everything I had wanted to see. The senioritas were all too lovely, and pondering! So with my backpack in hand and earphones blaring full volume, I stepped off the Greyhound Bus into downtown Denver, Colorado. I was now at the tender age of twenty-one, after a fifteen year separation from this city. I had not been back since my birth.

"Now if I can just find a payphone."

I whispered lowly to streetlights of the city, "I'll get around to you personally." With a smile on my face, I felt surge zero! This was ample enough fuel to power my new way to be.

"If I can meet a few little friends..." and with those thoughts in mind, I dialed my older cousin's telephone number.

After the first couple of rings, I felt

slightly nervous. If he didn't answer his phone, or if the number changed, I was headed to a wide, new world of confusion and a (first class) window seat to "stress land"! He then answered the phone after the 4th ring, which greatly reduced stress levels for me.

"Hey, Cuz, I finally made it here."

"A little Cuz. I'll be up there in a minute," he said.

I then proceeded along back to the bus station's seating area not too far from the door though. There was no way I was even chancing or missing my first day into this "old city" of mine. There was a pregnant woman that sat close to me; close enough to where an easy conversation was accessible.

"You ate?" she asked me. I thought to myself, "Am I that skinny?" Yes indeed though. I was every bit of 140 pounds soaking wet. Looking into my reflection off the window, I appeared skinny in such apparel of a yellow sun visor, one buttoned-down long sleeve shirt, an extra large pair of khaki pants with the pockets, a backpack, and a fresh split right above my left eyebrow.

Suddenly I realized that I didn't even know what kind of car to expect. So every car which got close to the smoking area where we sat sent anxiety and panicky pulses of adrenaline into my bloodstream! Everyone around me was apparently feeling the same. You could tell by their gazes. They as well, were anticipating their ride shortly.

The woman beside me looked as if she could have been hopping into the approaching 80's modeled B.M.W. It sure did pull up to the sidewalk curb with the windows decreasing in height, right around the area that we occupied. Surprisingly, the driver got out of the car and right into my new world! Alas, it was my cousin indeed, in the B.M.W. This was a very good sign of the livelihood ahead.

"Cuz go ahead and throw ya bags in the back," he said while approaching me for the family embrace of kinship. "Wus up lil' Cuz?" he said to me as we clasped hands for the single shoulder hug and smile. "Hop in and let's roll from up from here!" I heard him say, at the same time when he lit up a perfectly rolled Indo joint.

My own laughter clouded out any chance of doubts. I had made it thus far. I couldn't tell you that I saw familiar places, but what I did see was just as welcoming! The mountainous skyline set to the west side of the state, with their snowcaps and jagged structures underneath the clouds above them.

I pulled my sun visor down a little lower, and sat back a little farther in my seat. This was the last inch of a left-over smoke session. Though once I reached my cousin's place, I knew that many more were coming. Fifteen minutes into our journey, and I was convinced that I myself had to make my mark into his field of living.

This older cousin reflected years of

successful living. He had something that one really couldn't refer to as a nine to five. His life was based upon moonlight and streetlights, corners and nightspots, the bars and the pool halls! Ultimately speaking, pimping was how he slept. Pimping was how he awoke.

I myself being so undemonstrated to such a level of consciousness, quickly retracted all senses of what I had perceived as game - realizing that I had only now to observe and catch on during the process of transformation. I just had to add all of the past to the new.

The car was in very good condition, I acknowledged to myself. The engine purred softly, the sunroof moved, and the tires stuck to the road. The smoothness was even in the sudden accelerations to the breakings at the lights! The quick evenly maneuvered turns helped us get off and into the highway traffic.

The trees that lined the sidewalks were in their autumn stages. They were extraordinary! His neighborhood was mostly comprised of townhouses. Some of them were four-slot platforms. His townhouse was the one a little from the street corner.

As we pulled up, I saw two cars as well. One was a late model 64 - gold in color, with the brown and tan interior. The other one was a vehicle that looked as if it came out of a time capsule or something. It was blue and white and in perfect condition, maybe in the 50's model as far as I could tell.

"Cuz, both of those cars are mine," he said.

I wasn't shocked, for I had always known him to ride in major cars. After putting the car in park, he said, "Alright Cuz, we here."

I looked up at the steps that led to the apartment and saw a woman standing in the door. She was smoking, I could tell whilst grabbing my bags. I felt the weight of my life and the relief of this future, even as uncertain as it was.

Entering the apartment was none other than a stage I must have seen on at least a couple of movies I knew: The Mack, Super Fly, maybe Dolomite! Again, I can say I was religious at certain situations such as this cause all I could think was "Oh my God," and "Oh my goodness." I am not trying to say I was right with this, but during those times, I could most definitely appreciate the magnificence of creation!

"Hey, you can take ya bags in there. This where ya lil' room' at Cuz. I know ya tired and all, so we gonna rest up," he said.

I looked. I entered the side room and closed the shudder doors. I sat slowly down on the bed, which was one of the softest beds I'd ever seen! I looked out the window and over at the clock on the nightstand. I then opened my bags in some way, and placed out some form of decent attire for the (rise) tomorrow.

At every shirt and pair of jeans, there

hid a memory or detail of some sequence of a day in the many days of mighty Memphis, Tennessee. I was sick and sad, but all the while very much satisfied at my decision to move some couple of thousand miles from my home city. After a few minutes later, I rejoined my Cuz, and his female companions, sitting under the darkness of a movie atmosphere, looking out with Indo smoked visions. I sat along side of my Cuz about the couch area, just in time to retrieve the end piece to finish off!

What a sight, I thought as I saw my cousin rise from the couch with the gators and slacks attached to the shirt that probably was worth more than all I had. He rose to stretch, and his women began to display signs of retiring as well. Therefore, after extinguishing a cigarette, my cousin notified me that there was an abundant selection of movies to watch, or cable, and if I felt the need for refreshment, the beverages were in the kitchen and all.

"Alright Cuz, and thanks!" I said to him feeling the tiredness of the trip myself. On the television, I noticed how the news was different, and different music and sitcom selections.

I was a long, long, way from home, so how would I make money? Who would be my girlfriend? With whom would I socialize? How could I get my feet in the right direction? Where would I start?

My conscience questioned me. It seems

like the answers were all around me. I was now living with what it looks like to have power in the game! I would be drawing from it to provide a livelihood for one's self, and how fun it appeared to be.

It didn't take long to fall asleep once I lay back in the cool air of the mile high streets. I was worn-out by a 36-hour trip. How much must I see in that morning, daylight?

Immediately my senses of feelings alerted me to the fact that I was definitely in another bed! After that thought, joy and excitement rushed into my eager and rejuvenated body. On this particular sunrise, I wouldn't be walking outside to the same old business as usual. This day I would be on uncharted ground - extremely new and fresh ink!

The sounds of the television in the front room made me a bit nervous. Was it one of the women, I had seen yesterday, in some form of sleep attire? Was it my cousin adjusting to a new morning, preparing to roll up for the next session?

I dressed as appropriately as I could. Opening the doors showed me what getting up for a morning is supposed to be like!

In an exhale of smoke, Mac J. spoke out. "Ya sleep good Cuz-o?"

"Yeah man."

"Do you have something else to wear, Cuz?" he asked.

I ran down the few options of attire at

my discretion, but with a smile and a pass of the joint, he got up and told me he had some clothes that I could fit into. This wasn't a dream. This was how it was supposed to be; somebody looking out for a young, up and coming person like me. I knew that once I got on my feet I was to return the appreciation.

CHAPTER 9:
THE STACY ADAMS DAYS

Now a days, I could be seen in short sleeves, open collar, burgundy and silk shirt, nicely tucked inside my plaid, thin, long-stripped slack pants, with the size ten, black, low-ankle Stacy Adams. I'm riding sitting on the passenger side of the grey, sun-roofed B.M.W. pulling into the parking lot of some foreign western-style corner store.

Lo and behold, now who would have imagined? Maybe a new friend would! I opened the door, for I had spotted the first woman that returned my gaze of interest. She and I approached each other at the storefront.

"Hey, wus up lil' lady?" I asked the 5 ft.4 inches, 160-pound, dark skinned beauty with nice long black hair all the way to the scalp! She had a beaming smile and bright whites in her mouth. These gave grace to her brown tinted eyes.

We could be seen standing there with our mini-info transactions. We were now ready to leave the store. It was cool for I had every thing that I needed for the now prospect contact.

"I'll call you later, so you can swing by," I said to 'er.

"I'll be ready," she said in return, and walking away back to the car from which she sprang. We kept looking at each other. I knew then that I had better not mess that up.

"Cuz ya already making a lil' progress I see? But uh, what kind of situation are you gonna make of it?" I sat there listening to him. "If ya trying to come on down! You might as well come on out the door with what it is ya plan to do."

I listened, and knew that he meant for me to step immediately into the game. I wondered what would come of this. It didn't bother me though, for I was Memphis born!

Sure enough the very same day on the same evening as I sat on the couch enjoying a movie, I was also relaxing to the stress-free environment of this newly dwelling state of mind. I began to bare witness to the inside blood, bone, and structure of the game. Four young women of my Cousin's escort service sat nicely against a whole lot of other women that weren't as lively. So they indeed posed a threat to the household. One of them sat quietly in front of the computer, over-looking today's forecast of dating opportunities, while, another could be seen going back and forth about the other rooms with hair products and clothing.

Still, one more sat on the other couch across the room separating buds from stems, selecting the right amount for the next 1.5 syndrome. The clock showed me that yet so much was going on, it was still rather early. It was after the four-o'clock hour.

Reaching into my wallet, I took out the first number that I had gotten earlier from the store. My nerves were on edge, for I didn't know the elements of conversation used in this most distant state of Colorado, hundreds of miles from my own familiar Memphis stumping grounds. The phone and I stood suspended in air, before I dialed in the sweet intercession of what would bring me closer to such an establishment as his has shown clearly!

"Hello...is Khalikia there?" I asked whoever had answered the call.

"Yes, it is me."

I thought about hesitating, calling back, or just hanging up! But the pimp in me responded, "Hey...uh...I'm here! Think you can come on over?"

Every time I was outside, the scenery overwhelmed me. Off the top, there back in the distance of the lower sky and clouds, was the jagged borderline of mountains. It seemed as if they stood over the city. It looked as if they stretched across the entire state from that direction.

The trees here were different, as was the wildlife. Several cars went along on the street past the house, by which I stood about in the front yard. All of the cars continued, except this certain one. It passed me, went on along, and turned around only to come back into my direction.

My eyes began to squint to see past the evening sun, and later I brought them into full focus. I could see, emerging from the back seat of the car, the same dark hair, dark skinned, bright white, brown tinted eyes, beautifully toned skin young lady.

As she proceeded to climb from the back seat of the car, she had a little trouble. It seemed like the driver didn't seem to give the room needed for her to get out. Then sure enough, with the door open and herself nearly completely out of the vehicle, the door edge caught her with a thudding along the side of her face. It was a nice blow, I thought somewhat remorsefully. She didn't seem to even notice, for she once again was looking straight at me. On her way towards me, I found myself thinking, "lil' lady, if ya knew what I had in mind, you would break and run!" But then again, my smile and voice responded, "Why hello, again!"

"So how is it that I'm a perfect stranger here?" jokingly said, of course. "Maybe you can help re-familiarize me with this old city of mine," is how my conversation began with the now elegantly dressed woman, in the long, black, waist-hugging dress.

"I can do that for you. Whatever you want. I can do it for you. I got cha! How long have you been here? Your accent really got my attention ya know. When I saw you, I knew you weren't from around here."

As I stood there and listened to her, I felt inside that if I weren't money hungry, ya know, I probably could have fallen for a lovely woman as such, as she was. I could see us getting together for movies, going out to restaurants, maybe even settling down in an apartment together - the straight family life perhaps! Then again, there was the well-known fact that we would be entering the house soon, so the lifestyle that she was to see off the intro, was none other than the street life.

"Let's gone on in, so I can introduce you to the others," I said to 'er, letting her hand go. The hand linked us together for that brief bout to be non-existent boyfriend and girlfriend duo. The steps that led us inside would be the first in a long, long, relationship with the sidewalks, the pavement, and the nightlife walking.

I had braids in my hair but she undid those and began to implement her own craftiness. All the while, she was talking to me in that unforgiving black, Mexican-mix lingo, touching my face and arms. She moved her hands along my chest area, and whispered to me that she'd like to take me into one of the non-occupied rooms for just a few minutes at least.

I really didn't expect her to fall for me the way she appeared to be doing. Thoughts crossed my mind such as "Did she expect a relationship?" "How would she be with me considering how I had planned to get by?"

"Hey, look here, say tomorrow perhaps, is you willing and able enough to get out with ya man? Are you one-hundred percent with me? Are you confused as in you don't understand me and the life that I chose to live?" I asked her while dropping the ashes from my cigarette.

"I got you. I'm ah be with you. Of course, I'll go with you! I'm not trying to leave ya side if I can help it," was her response to me.

"Hey, Cuz! You and the lil' lady get ready. We 'bout to ride out," Mac yelled down to me from the upper part of his house.

After she had finished my hair, she took a few seconds to observe her handiwork - rubbing down the sides of my head.

"The weather changes so fast," I commented while looking out the front door on our way out of the house. "It's actually snowing now, and all from a sunny day?" I asked.

She replied, "Yes, it is. But tomorrow this little snowfall will be gone like it never was there."

Maybe it should snow tomorrow I felt. It

would spare her the all too real reality of our destiny for sure!

Tomorrow came. Oh, boy was I nervous! What a situation at hand! I'd never been this close to going so deep down in this game, and then again so fast at that! I didn't even know where to begin. None of the movies in the world could help me once the reality of hunger and shelter set down around me.

I had another cousin who also stayed on the corner intersection of a very busy highway. From her apartment steps, I saw traffic all the way up and down Colfax, through all times of the day and night. You could see the bus stops, the neon-liquor store signs, and I kept thinking secretly that they would be of some use to me.

The corner stores, the fast food joints, and more than all others, the hotel spots were on every other lot or so. I looked across the table at my meal ticket, and noticed that she still had the same gaze of interest, no signs of breakage, no signs of doubt, and absolutely no sense of the event yet to come.

"40 dollars for a room, but a hundred dollars is breakfast," I said to 'er.

Here was no more time for make-believe, for the very breakfast that we ate was over ten dollars, and I was down to the last twenty, knowing that the other things I had to purchase were a pack of Newport and a box of our, all-trusting condoms. I lit one of the last three Newports. So that left me with two more reasons for us to go ahead and see what the business was like.

By looking after her, I knew that I had better save one of the condoms for myself. But the other two, most definitely would have to equal up to a hundred dollars apiece. That meant two hundred dollars; by the time we were to get a room for the evening. After paying the waitress and a small tip, we exited the spot, only to stand right out front, on the sidewalk.

I lit another cigarette and told 'er straight up, "First thing, I'm going to walk to the store. I want you to wait a few minutes." After saying that, I took a few seconds for study. "After I pass you, plus a block or so, just follow on from behind."

I extended my hand to give her the remainder of the cigarette I had almost smoked completely, at the same time looking deep into her eyes. I was almost, almost hesitant, because she was indeed lovely enough to entrap a man right toward a normal lifestyle. Then again, my eyes shifted on toward the traffic flow. It was getting a little busy. Seeing that it was close to twelve o'clock, it was best to get going considering that the traffic would swell even more due to lunch being so close.

With all procrastination aside, it was time for action! I left her standing there, only turning back for a look, and a slight smile of motivation. She still had no traces of cowardness. She only pulled back her hair to the back, then after another drag on the square, thumped it away, mixing with the whirlwinds of traffic.

And I'll be damned. No sooner had I made it out of the store, I saw her talking to the first Joe! As I noticed, it was an affair! I made haste toward the vehicle, making it to the slightly cracked passenger window just in time to drop a box of condoms successfully into her lap.

I was panicking now in a way that I had never done before. Thoughts like "Would she make it back safely?" "How long was it going to take?" crossed my mind repeatedly. Man, I felt I needed a drink for sure. I spotted the first liquor store not far from where we were. I was on the other side of the street, thereby cautiously, I made way to the other side, looking behind me every few steps, looking for witnesses (or) the cops!

A smile of confidence set down across my lips, and a darker me was arising, not by spirit, for I loved the game, but by perception! Seeing it happen so soon let me know right then, that we could be working well into most nights.

With four dollars to spare, I purchased a 2-dollar bottle of dark eyes vodka, and dreamed about my meeting with the dope man! After a little searching around my pocket for maybe a dime to go with the two 1-dollar bills, I paid the man behind the glass window. Then after retrieving my half-pint of cold drank I suddenly felt the rush of what was actually going on. I was doing what it was that I had seen on the all-famous movies.

I was reflecting the image of my older cousin's instruction, and I bet if he saw me, he'd be very proud! It had been at least thirty minutes since I had last seen my girl, and again I wondered about what was going on. So out of the store I headed, and back towards where we had last seen each other. I was a nervous wreck, let me tell you! I twisted the seal off the bottle and took a couple of quick squibs before reseal. It was getting darker now and the sun began to set behind the mountains. All of these things being so new to my eyes, I walked toward a Dixie Queen and thought to go ahead in and maybe have a bite to eat.

Sure enough, on down the line in the distance, maybe a streetlight or so from where I was, I saw the figure of my champion approaching. She was walking speedily towards me. I got somewhat spooked! When we got close enough, it was nothing but smiles between us. In her hand were a few bills of some sort rolled up real nice like.

No man could tell me shit! Right there at that time, she most definitely did the damn thang, and returned to me placing in my hand five twenty dollar bills, and in the other hand the remaining condoms. I scolded her slightly, right then, and there, for placing money in my hand out there in the open. Sure enough, it was all said and done, with a picture of a perfect smile. Then I felt it was time for me to introduce myself to her physically.

After all, she did prove worthy. A good hot bath and soap would remove all skepticism of me touching her. I had definitely planned to do that. She started talking about what went on with the (Joe), and strange things were said, I might add.

We had just pulled the first hundred dollar though. There was a hotel a few meters from the Dixie Queen. I had intended on stopping by earlier. Looking at her breathing and over-excitement, I remembered that we both could use some food and conversation. Celebration would fit our first night together. So from behind her I suggested the above plan. So together, we walked on up the lot to inside the restaurant. Everything on the menu was up for grabs now, as I thought shortly to myself how only just a few minutes ago, I couldn't afford too much at all.

My choices were like one burger, and just maybe some fries, if they had mercy still. I got a small cup of ice water as well. It was joy when I perceived how after only an hour my choices broadened ten times, and no other feeling was like it.

From behind, I observed closely as she explained what she wanted from the cashier, also noticing the hotel lights. They were ne-to-the-on! Looking at my champion, I thought gleefully, "Man oh man, a memphizz nigga iz in the house! WOW!"

CHAPTER 10:
THE STREET LIFE

Only just earlier today, we sat at the restaurant and spoke of these things. Who would believe, that in all actuality we both took to the street life like fish to water! Matter of fact being, I had only been here twelve days and this is what I got!

All kinds of urges came, and I desired to call down to my hometown to spread the news to my family and friends. Yet and still I thought, who would believe me? Thinking perhaps it might be beginners luck, I considered otherwise. Whatever it was that was happening, it was most definitely indeed happening.

So with food in hand now and the evening settling in, I looked into what it was that was made and went ahead and subtracted 40 dollars for the room. Checkout time was at 11:00 A.M.

"So what's up?" she said as the remnants of her food lay there on her tray.

"How about we take this on in for tonight, ya know? How about we spend our first night together? It will be our first time alone together. Are you ready for that?" I said to her as she sat there wiping her fingertips, and licking the rest of food particles from her mouth.

In the same thought was the fact that she had just really had sex. How did I feel about that? I mean my girl was with another man less than an hour ago. Was I cool with it...like, is this alright? Yes indeed, for this girlfriend of mine got money for the occasion, real quick, and the money is in my pocket.

"Yeah lady, let's go and check in the room for you to get situated, and I'll go to my cousin's house to get some Bud real quick." Smiling now, we got up to leave, and I still followed from behind 'er, looking at that ass!

The Chinese man behind the hotel counter asked me for my I.D. This was nothing strange, for I had come across a few hotels in my time. After examination, he simply acknowledged that the room would be 40 dollars for the night. I paid him, and while putting away my wallet my peripheral vision was soaking up the image to my immediate left, informing me by looks and body, it most definitely was going to be an interesting night!

The clock ticked on past 9:00 P.M. and we instantly, with no more procrastination made our way to room 104. With key in hand and a few twists of the wrist, I unlocked a full night of some of the.... a young man could encounter. Let me spare you the details.

With the awkwardness of silence, the sounds of thunder could be heard across the busy city night, right there outside our hotel room. It was only 12:00 midnight. Mac J. did hip me to the fact that the nights were good business, but at the same time, very, very risky!

Now after an ignited flame and a glowing orange tip in the dark, I exhaled the sigh of relief. The relief of being fed and under shelter, all on our own. This new strange city of my youth and the mile high streets as they called them sure did look out for a "Westwood, Memphis, Tennessee, drugged up, liquorized, 21 yr. old fellow like me!"

To be honest with you, all I knew was that when you are outside walking, someone is going to eventually notice, especially if they're interested. This was the only motivation I had to go on. Well, not the only one, for we both had cigarettes, weed, drinking habits, plus maybe a few more behind closed doors.

The morning light began to put away the night, and the anticipation of the phone ringing for us to check out made me think deep and hard. In honesty this was most dangerous what we were enacting. This could have caused us to lose freedom, or maybe even our lives.

But I had nothing else going. What else were we supposed to do being out in the darkness of a most intimidating dog-eat-dog game? I rose earlier than she did. I let her rest. Her body would need it.

Her breathing was steady, as she lay under the covers nude and unsuspecting. Oblivious to the fact that really, I wasn't her shining knight, or Romeo, and I wasn't interested in marriage. Still, I truly and surely was her escort into this trivial game of survival.

On the other hand, before she met me, I could tell that she was doing the damn thang. Then again maybe it was just for pleasure. Now she had seen the machinations of a trick and how they could give like a cow, and it was sweet. I could feel that she knew this.

"Hey, let's wake up, and get dressed. We got breakfast to tend too and plenty to roll." I could see the semi-smile on her lovely face, and I'm thinking to myself, "We got a real winner here!"

I sat on the couch for about 30 minutes. That's about the amount of time it took her, to get it together. We didn't bother to extend our time on something as tiresome as sex. We went ahead and checked out of the room at least an hour before scheduled time.

It was a cool, lovely Wednesday morning. I still got chills as in how much more advanced and high paced this city was, all to the advantage though! On entering the office, the hotel assistant gladly received our key and remote control. The return of the remote control meant a two-dollar return.

There was a spot across the street medium from us. We both could use a major breakfast before the start of the day. Our friends, the Mexicans, ran the place. As we walked through the front doors the Senorita that greeted us was very nice indeed!

As my girl and I ordered our food, we pretty much felt the same way I suppose about what was actually going on. Yeah this was no joke! But let me tell you though, the price of our food meant that we were definitely in the game.

By the time we finished scrambled eggs and toast, with the cofee, plus my French toast and omelets, along with a couple cups of coffee, we needed to come up with enough stamina to withstand such a humid mid-day morning. Already we had smoked half the pack of cigarettes, meaning whatever was depleting in supply needed replacing A.S.A.P.

"You know uh, yesterday went fairly well seeing that it was our first time out. We made enough for bed and breakfast sure, as we got that earlier yesterday. The same potential awaits us today!" I said to her in a low tone. Her looks and medium build was the motivation of the perception, that in no time at all we could get far ahead in the games! I felt the adrenaline surge vibrate through my soul. With an extinguishment of the third cigarette, it was time to go.

"I'm going to go to the restroom. I'll be right back!" the charming little whore said to me.

She had better hurry up; I sensed to myself, feeling as her mini sundress disappeared after fifteen steps across the room. I was already at the register as in the same time she had returned. She must have moistened up her hair a bit too, cause just before it was a little on the "she just rose up off a pillow" kind of look going on.

The cashier took the 20-dollar bill giving me the change all in a matter of seconds, and believe me, every dollar was as good as a hundred dollars. Meaning it was extraordinarily complicated to earn this kind of money in the most crucial of games. We have seen that there were no guarantees. Something could shake on every stroll down the avenue.

I couldn't help but to feel nervous as we exited the restaurant. The cars and trucks right off the very sidewalk were roaring past us. The wind off the vehicles shook both of our hair-dos. But still she and I proceeded to unlock the strategy of maybe another catch, then again maybe an escape route.

"Alright now," I said to 'er. "This is Colfax, right?"

She responded with a yes. Then I gave her a couple of pointers as how the police patrolled it, faithfully!

"Well you and I can't let the traffic miss too much of us. Whatever it may be. Besides, last night was just the beginning. We have other avenues!" This I had to believe, because so far I was just walking on faith.

I'd walk about two lights ahead listening to D.J. Paul on my earphones. The music made me feel somewhat closer to home. Sometimes, I'd get so down, into one of the songs, I'd forget my surroundings. I would forget the fact that I was at least a thousand miles away. After a few minutes had past, I'd cautiously walk to the nearest payphone to rest a bit, also to see how close or far apart we were.

I didn't have too much change to waste on calls. So mostly I'd go through the motions and pretend to talk to someone while I held the phone to my ears. My intensions really were to watch the passer-bys, and with passion, watch the faces and body language of would-be customers.

The feelings of accomplishment out-weighed the slum anticipation of waiting. My smile could be seen from light-years away, meaning we had another vehicle to pull over along the side street. This meant two things, I would head back to the meeting place to await her return, and secondly make a trip back to my cousin's house to re-up.

"Man, I hope she gets back safe, soon, and as sexy as she was when I last saw her," I mumbled into the earlier morning breeze. Those words became a slick prayer so to speak, knowing that there weren't too many blessings in this line of business. It's strange, but also it's survival.

"The Late Night Tip" track was on, and I turned it up to max or to whatever my small headphones could put out. It seems as if the instrument and my footsteps were in perfect harmony. I'm talking pure Memphis vibe in those cold, dark, mile-high Colorado streets!

"This most definitely is the life, for thiz nigga here," I said rather laughingly, and quick stepping, always looking up and around me, noticing the area. I had to still notice the dare devil traffic. After hours of treading their city blocks and side-street sidewalks, I could perceive that this was a traffic line combo of every nationality.

We weren't discriminating as we made our way down the avenue. Colfax was one of the longest streets in the United States. People actually pointed that out to me! They told me one day, that it covered almost three whole states!

I crossed the intersection. and I could notice a familiar area now. I recognized the all-famous Star Motel. The neon signs were out! I began thinking to myself gladly that in a few more hours we'd be kicked back, watching the TV, running bath water, rolling sun, and taking shots all at the same time.

With those thoughts, I walked up to my

older cousin Channel's apartment door only to notice through their window, a scene of them, the liquor, and a few interesting friends of hers. Channel had two young sons, and they really could stir up my spirits at times. Upon entering the doorway, I could hear their high proper dialectic conversation.

"Hey wus up Cuz? J. just left here! He said that he'd be back later on tonight or something."

I asked the older one of the two "How long has he been gone?" Both of them tried to answer me at the same time, leading to one of their many arguments. I was just smiling at them, because they reminded me a lot of me and my own brother, coming up through the eighties, and late seventies indeed! Those most terrific times, those golden years of youth seemed to pass by faster after the reality that there were no more toys to be received for Christmas.

I also began to notice their relationship to the parents! Nevertheless, man, look at where I am. I'm caught up, in a world of chaos, slowly anticipating the worst, but trying my best to get to the better. I took a seat in the living room, and began to mingle a bit. Besides, I had a little over an hour before my girl was expected to be on the rise.

Reaching into my pocket was a slick joy these last couple of days! There was the fact that, at one time or another on any given occasion, the contents of my pocket could get the average black man a couple of years easily. But thus far, I retrieved my cigarettes, the fresh Newports! The pack of cigarettes in a house like ours, or rather my kinfolks', could go fast! I mean, with a six-pack of beer, 15 squares were smoked, give or take a couple. You damn near had to go for a walk to smoke the whole thing! I had no problem with that though, because after all the above said, I'd be the first to say, "Cuz, let me get a square!"

Every card game was filled with yelling, cursing, and cigarette dumping. Did I mention cigarette thumping? I could play maybe spade or something like a couple other basic games. But these fools were into all of them, so I mostly just sat back and drank, then used the telephone from time to time.

"Hey, um, so you my cousin's friend?" I asked one of the women that sat amongst us. "Now you know me so wus up wit us?"

She said nothing. She only smiled agreeing.

At this point, I wanted to ask all the haters to exit the premises! Anyway, the conversation with ole girl was a successful one. But man, I thought, if she stays here any longer, she'll be pissed, or she'll be awed! I thought about it, and how she would respond to the way in which I chose to conduct relationships.

"Hey, walk to the store with me," my Cuz Mac J. was telling me from contact, just passing each other in the hallway. After grabbing my jacket, I told the woman friend of mine that we would soon return.

Upon leaving the apartment, I then thought of the traffic, and the amount of time it had been since me and Kahlikia had last seen each other. We had walked familiar routes these last few days, so I knew where I would eventually run into her. The steps were used so much everyday, going in and out of the apartment complex that we could have walked 'em blindfolded! But who would do that with such lovely mountains in the yonder skyline and as I, and my cousin walked, I felt the urge for a bottle of vodka coming on!

"Hey Cuzzo, where ya lady at?" he asked me as we made it around the apartment complex on our way to the sidewalk. This sidewalk lined one of the busiest streets in North America.

"Well Cuz, me and her got out earlier today. She'll be back shortly I hope. I'm telling ya Cuz, every time she leaves my side, I'm damn near a nervous wreck!"

After those words, my lips silenced, due to the entrance of my 4th cigarette from the pack. "I might end up taking a stroll once we leave the store. Know what I'm saying?" He nodded in agreement.

I couldn't do nothing but admire the fellow. He was dealing with day-to-day situations with that crazy-ass cousin of mine. The average everyday hustlers were a constant sight around the corner store, posted also at the bus stops, looking obviously devious, even to the untrained eye. But who was I to judge? A couple of them were familiar to me. Some would see me checking in and out of the room with my girl, and there was a slick hint of respect in the air.

After purchasing a few goodies, we exited the store. "Hey Cuz, I'm gonna catch up in a few." With that, I gazed down the mid evening traffic, full of adrenaline. The air was feeling somewhat neat!

I was very careful not to look directly at the suspicious vehicles that passed because I most definitely didn't want any unnecessary attention! The fact was that every minute out there, was one minute too long!

"Dang! This here ain't gonna work right here," I mumbled with my teeth barely parting. After crossing Peoria off Colfax, I went ahead and used the payphone to let 'em know that I'd probably be there later. At this time, and after being up there for a while, I learned that close attention is to be paid while dialing numbers. There weren't any quarters to waste out there, with no cell phone handy!

My cousin Rochelle herself answered the phone and she was "crunk"! I could hear it in her laughter before she said hello. "Aye wus going on Cuz?" she responded with the same greeting. "Aye Cuz, ya girl just got back. She is standing out on the steps." After I heard those words, I quickly got off the phone after two or three more words. Now the downhill tread was in motion, and my nerves eased up. I felt confidence growing inside me. It was stunning!

The streets were golden in my eyes! Let me explain. Out of every 25 to 50 cars, there'd be men watching, and some would slow down turning off onto a side street. Some honked their horns, but for us, the very best of 'em actually got involved.

Yet like that old saying goes, (all that glitters ain't Gold!) Yeah see, in those cars, that we were intensely concerned about, some were police, some were detectives, and some were even psychos. We had them all mixed in together. It was our lunch tray! Some things on the plate were not digestible.

By the time I got to the Rochelle's apartment, it was just about sunset. I remembered the one new, lady-friend with whom I was socializing. My heart rate increased when I thought of the situation at hand, but it felt good all the same. Man, what a long way from home I thought gladly!

I now was within one block from my destination. Before getting to that place, I would have to cross by a liquor store! Yeah man, if anyone needed a drink It would be me. Reaching into my pocket cost me another unnecessary cigarette, for by the time I got up to the apartment door I could hear a party going. My girl wasn't outside, thus meaning; maybe the opposite was in effect. Maybe she was inside along with that new friend of mine. I wondered.

Not everyone in the front room, fit the description I was looking for, but I spoke immediately. It was all love, and I was feeling ever the greater. I could see and think to myself again. Let me scope my new girl and hold her down, I was thinking.

With a glance of familiarity, I did the "I'm going to holler at 'cha" kind of gesture. The kitchen light alerted me to my prime suspect of interest! As I walked into the kitchen, she almost instantly turned to see. "She!" had that "Um relax 'cause I been a good girl" type of expression on her face! I then knew that once more, our night and morning would be treated as damn near royalty, messing around with a hundred dollars every few hours or so!

We joined everyone else in the front. I had a nice seat and resumed the formal introduction sequence of action that familiarizes individuals from the start. In other words, you could tell that we would be kicking it soon!

With my attention back to my partner in crime, 'my champ', I looked at 'er and told 'er that we would need a room soon. She still held the money in her hand! So I knew she felt good about the catch, what a monster!

It was now almost 9:30 P.M. The three of us had been sitting together for almost two hours. Might I say, a little progress might be an understatement. Within that period I had gotten a room and posted my girl there to shower, get her hair together and to roll something for us, for the time that I was to return. That gave me, and my newest friend, time to chop it up personally!

She had a younger son. He was like 9. She had her own apartment and she sold rocks! So I began thinking things like, "That'll be my smoking spot. That'll be my hideaway, during the earlier morning hours, or hot times! Of course, last but not least, I think it would be best if she became a part of our little shin-dig!"

"So you ain't got a problem with how my thing goes?" I asked.

"No problem, hommie. If ya wanna come over sometime, we can chill out together."

After the small talk outside, I let her walk ahead of me, and again I felt a slick sorrow for another unsuspecting, willing, and an opportunist type of young lady. I was opening the door to the party, and at the same time, a door of another opportunity.

"Man, where in the world did I get the keys?" I wondered in all honesty.

CHAPTER 11:
THE NEW GIRL

I'll tell you this; two things had to happen in the mornings out in the lovely city of Aurora, Colorado. I'm talking straight hood! That part of town was at least 80% Mexican! There were Asians as well. Everyday though was "crunk"! One thing was most apparent. Regardless of the differences of nationality, our laughter sounded the same. Waking up early was usually the case. Coffee could be counted on. It was our happy way of sitting up early, deciding which way our days could go!

I woke up to the sound of mother and children being correctec. L.B. and his brother Glen were having it out. They were fighting and saying disruptive things to one another! I guess they were no worse than me and my brother, I suppose. Where was the sun I wondered?

"Hey wus up Cuz?" They only smiled, knowing that the devious one hadn't gone to sleep at a conceivable time. I looked at the time. The party had been over for like a few hours now. I gained my senses and checked the contents of my pockets.

I was straight. I had ole girl's number, and the same amount of money and cigarettes! But damn, I thought instantly, I'd better get on over to the room!

I was somewhat frustrated, but I guess I did need a little catnap before returning to the clutches of that 19-year old fireball of Joy!

The nightlife was fantastic! They were only felt by the ones that appreciated the shade and non-occupancy of vision. The streetlights here and there were all the light that we required. Just feeling the cool mountain air rush past our mouths and noses was pure amplification of soul!

It was like I had been living on the block my whole life by the way I jumped the fences that separated the apartments from one another. It was nothing for me to be hitting the side alleys leading to unoccupied streets. It was simple crossing the 4-lane traffic at the corners, and seeing always, the other people on hot pursuit to the closest dollar bill that they've preyed upon. I was also always seeing the smokers with the necessary amount of money for their escapades!

I had only to cross over one more street

before I was at our room. I ain't going to lie; I was feeling kind of slum after such a twenty-hour stretch.

A car passed me right after I stepped onto the sidewalk into safety. It was so close. I wanted to flip the driver the finger! But the room's light that I saw still on, eased all the tension from one spirit to another. I knocked once. She asked who it was. I responded. Then she opened the door. Y'all pretty much know the rest.

She looked good and refreshed! She looked as if she was still moist from the bath or shower. Her skin was smooth as silk with a rich, dark-brown glow. She held a Newport, and by looking at it, she had only just lit it a couple of minutes ago. It was mine of course. For in this line of understanding, you didn't ask for the short, for in no way could you implant seeds of misdirection.

"Hey love, turn the A.C. on for a minute," I asked of 'er. We really appreciated the engineering team, for the mini-Antarctic A.C., in the midst of such a steaming hot relationship! I glanced at the table and saw a few more twenties. She must have turned another trick while I was on my kinfolk's floor, unresponsive, from oblivious amounts of Tequila, vodka, and beer! Taking a seat at the table, and taking off my shoes was the next stage, all while keeping my eyes on such a sacrificial membership!

"See what movie is on, and I'll get back

with you after I take a shower," I said to 'er while extinguishing the end of the square.

"And turn off the A.C., fo' a nigga' be coughing out tha azz." It was a humorous comment, not too long ago. I hadn't smiled as much! Now a-days, I could be seen with the semi-satisfied smile.

As I stood at the bathroom sink, the person in the mirror looked a lot different from the one that I remembered down state. The person that I now saw, looked a bit healthier. It could it be that the absence of certain drugs due to unfamiliar territory were having its affect. I confess it was healthier I thought, while rubbing the bottom part of the beard. It was all good perhaps, but still in the back of my head I could already see a fresh supply, with a new bottle before me, set neatly upon a table.

Who was I kidding? For with the first chance I got I had no self-control. I knew that I would get wasted, real quick and for all the right reasons I thought. Just about any occasion suited me just fine.

From as far as I could tell, the tub appeared to be clean, but I also kept in mind the many bodies that had emerged in sexual activity or what not, and everyone before us, attempting to cleanse themselves from whichever sin in which they may have indulged. Even so, a seemingly white tub was good enough for me; and with those thoughts, I adjusted the cold water and slowly added on the hot as well. In the background, I could hear my girl selecting tonight's movie feature.

"Goodness gracious," I said proudly, whilst shaking the hot water from my fingertips.

I asked 'er to bring me a square, so I could check her state of mind. She was alright I suppose; her timid smile was still intact. Her appearance hadn't changed other than the fact that I could see a lot more of her body.

"Open the peach soda for me." She responded by way of the sounds that are made that went along with such an operation.

Later the traffic could be heard all through the night. It was a good sign! It told me that it could go down at any time of day or night. Sometimes I could admit to myself that there indeed were panic times, and anxiety attacks. The very pressure of it made it hard to arise in the mornings after a late night.

I wondered was I making a horrible mistake leaving my hometown. I wondered about lying low tomorrow, just to chill out in the room? Punking out wasn't in my blood. But I did indeed have ultra sonar for trouble detection and by no way could I have perceived a life surrounded by what I hate to talk!

With the hot, soapy towel to my face, I focused as clear as I could, trying to spring thoughts from a mind such as mine! However, as I have said and will say again, a "Memphis boy was in the house!"

You could hear a mixture of the birds, the morning traffic, and maybe after a little anticipation, you would hear the checkout call soon afterwards. The tug of responsibility kept me from resuming sleep. There was a decent remnant of the blunt from last night that would do just fine! Sitting up, to ignite alerted her to my awakening. She moved a bit to adjust her position in a manner of an anticipated angle to receive or communicate.

"Hey lady, wus up?"

She laid there smiling as a response. I could see that she knew what my days and evenings were just about like! I couldn't tell if she had regrets though, might I add. It would make it easier for us by use of the buses today, because - uh – we most definitely were the newest faces on the strip. The sunlight wasn't as bright today as it had been earlier this week. I appreciated the cooler temperatures.

Breakfast was maybe the best next move before too long. That always sent chills through our bones. She sat up in the bed. Nudity wasn't a concern it seems ever for the lil' lady of mine!

She sure could motivate me with her support of character portrayal, and my determination. It was already reasoned best to have an early day, as early as possible. I figured my girl could use a little help I supposed!

Again we were well into our morning. I was already outside at the motel office, ready to return the key, while she waited in the parking lot, preparing for our departure to the newest favorite breakfast spot! I felt inside the urge to smoke a cigarette to calm the arising feelings of anxiety, the pressure. I went ahead and decided that last night was our last time at this particular motel.

Sure as it was back home, the same devices that people conjure to wreck ya day or night, was still an existing reality, even all the way up here. Since I could barely understand the men my age out here, I rarely was conversant with them. For this reason, they grew enviously curious. I spotted a couple of familiar faces as I had seen the other day, but only this time, they appeared untrustworthy! They did not have the same vibes as before. This I could feel one-hundred percent.

When I was at the age of 14, I decided that I would no longer use handguns. I was a lot older now and had seen a whole lot more. So the weight of the brass knuckles in my pocket evened the odds I felt!

"The buses have already passed us a few times. We'll get on the next one. I'll sit at the back. You go ahead and get off once we get to Kingston. I'll get off a few streets after and make my way back up!"

The bus came to a stop, and we entered according to plan. We followed the course of action, and after a couple of minutes she got off, and I too after a couple more streets. Looking toward where I last saw her, I could almost decipher her. I knew that money making stroll was a half a mile away!

The strange thing about this street was that after you passed one of the avenues farther down, you would be in an altogether different city. If I got off the bus on Kingston, and walked across the street to Dayton, I would be in Denver! I had only to cross back to leave it. Wow!

That only meant watching out for the cops in two cities at the same time. The area toward downtown was busier. There were more service stations, grocery stores, and a few more liquor stores. Then there was the Golden Domed building. I think it had something to do with their court system. They probably got a lot of money from their task forces about the streets. I took daily notes of that for references. The area was swarming with activity. I felt like maybe tonight we'd get a room on this side of Colfax! It was a kind of camp-out where the most action seemed to occur.

It was past two in the afternoon. This seemed like the right time for rooming arrangements. The sign wasn't on, but the bright bulbs spelled out "Star Motel". It looked decent enough. An hour had almost passed since our separation, so I knew that maybe things were on track right then! It really only took thirty minutes or so to catch a trick. This I've seen time and time again.

The grocery store was across the street from our future room, therefore the food would be easily attainable. There was an apartment complex right across from where we'd be later. There were people standing out. "My Johns" started kicking in. Every street person knew that if you weren't from around there, you really couldn't just walk up and inquire about certain areas, especially drug-related material! But at that point, none of that applied to me.

There were sections of this complex, and the majority of what I saw was inhabited by Mexicans. Maybe here or over there one would see someone other than that. Immediately they began to set their gazes upon me, and my vibe of unfamiliarity. Anyone else probably would of turned around, but this wasn't one of those people!

Since some of them looked like they were around my age group, I figured they already assumed a reason by which I was approaching them. I even hoped that maybe one of them would be prepared.

"Hey, what's up!" were the first of my words and I was cautious about keeping my hands away from my pockets, and never did I pull them toward my backside. From that, I guess they could tell that I was no way cop-related. I guess they could see the darkness in and around my eyes.

I felt that a couple of them, who stood there, might have gotten on too! I could see it in their eyes as well. I guess everything was alright, for they led me into the building. I was fully taken care of with absolutely no problem. That meant that tonight, everything was going to be "hectic" for it had been a couple of eons since I last "got down"!

The time had come for me to look for my girl. Off I walked on toward the street, only looking back to thank my new Amigo friends!

Boy was I bumping and crunking with the Playa-Fly like I had just heard of him! Now I felt my fangs, or dogteeth, because now I was a beast on foot. The only thing that kept me from feeling just as better as before, was the fact that I would have to walk up this hot street until I found my girl, and this, I prayed would happen soon.

She probably would have to watch out a lil' bit tonight. I had no interest in being out there. Plus sex would have to wait 'cause uh, the interest in that wasn't as intense.

After walking for about fifteen minutes further, I thought it best to go ahead and make a liquor store stop. I had a feeling that soon afterwards, I would see my girl on 'er way, simple fact, we had been over the procedure in order to iron out areas of confusion. I twisted the top to unlock the next stage of my evening, with three solid gulps, back to the twist on, and with a scan down the avenue I felt joy! Sure enough, I could tell that walk from anyone else in the City. That walk came with nerve, bountiful pure courage of heart, and the sexiness of her loyalty, all in one supreme package!

It looked as if she caught sight of me as well. I could see that she too was relieved to see me again. With me she had witnessed what it is not to 'starve' but to succeed. I only acknowledged that I saw her by crossing over to the other side of the street. My intensions were to walk back down to the new room, leading her on down the avenue. I didn't want to be seen as a couple to the onlookers or the suspects. Plus, before getting to our spot there could be another fellow to pull over or something of the sort.

I preferred that we got on to the room though. There was a Subway restaurant in front of us, and I knew it was time to feed thiz bitch! (Pardon my Dutch). On the entrance into Subway, I immediately was on the counter like "Let me get the meatball with cheese on wheat, pronto!" I was the kind of person that chose not to get involved in conversation whilst having food prepared, so my English was used precisely. When the door opened behind me I rather figured that it was she, and I was happy of course with another successful adventure, I suppose. Behind me she stood, looking in good condition and high in spirits. I turned to look at 'er, with a smile beneath my nose!

"Hey lady, we gonna head on down to the spot." She heard me and felt better I suppose. With that, she ordered her 12-inch turkey and ham sandwich, while I walked out to smoke thus another Newport!

My sandwich was warm next to my leg. I knew that I would enjoy that meal, "as soon as she came the hell on," thought.

She stepped out the door just in time to get the short of the cigarette. I looked at 'er very carefully - her complexion and her curves - a shame that such a lovely young lady had gone astray! Her hair hung down her back most of the time, and it had a reddened brown kind of tint to its ends.

"We probably are just going to sit back and watch movies for a while." With saying those words there was no further need really to stand there. Following my lead she began her walk as well, but now with readiness for we had a secure spot, and my guess was that she'd probably be wanting to get a little closer than normal around about this time of day! There were a couple of streets to go before getting to spot A. I heard a couple of car horns maybe a couple of teenagers perhaps! Customers didn't give themselves away that easily. My intensions were to get back to the room as safe as possible.

I turned around to look before crossing the street, and be about the business! Someone had pulled up and onto the side street. I motioned to her that the hotel was clearly in sight, and that I would be there waiting for her return. That situation made me walk on up to the room and into it feeling like a million bucks! I had my liquor, my cigarettes, my sandwich, and a nice lil' something extra! I organized all the items neatly on the table, for it was about to go down.

It had been like an hour and a half, so

by now my nerves were on fire! It didn't help that since I had been there, I had gotten loaded and fully intoxicated. The cigarette butts began to out-number the cigarettes I had left in the box! It had gotten to the point now that I'd smoke half, putting the rest out for later; at the same time, constantly looking out the window blinds.

Picking up the bottle, I had a little less than half the vodka now, and it was way-too early in the evening. I knew that I would have to make at least one more visit, not to mention the fact that along the way, it would be clean cross the very apartment complex that kick-started the madness of mine!

After sitting still for a few minutes to let my heart rate succumb down to an appropriate speed, I reached for the room key. I really didn't feel like going anywhere to be totally honest, but, in this game, laziness could mean an eviction, or worst off eating nothing at all in a city like this. Never the less, I counted what we had collected these last few hours after deducting the room fair and all other necessities for a young couple like ourselves.

Moreover, in a city as hot as this, you learn to strike and hide! The consequences could be bad if greed tinted perceptions of the dangers that lurked.

One thing I noticed here was that even names were different up here! Down south, you'd have names like Tonya, Tameka, and Keisha. Up here, there were names such as

Shy, Slinkier, and Deloris - ones of that nature. Yet, from off the little list I had, I choose to call up the one I had contact with over at my cousin's house the other day. She probably would ask me why it had taken so long for me to contact 'er. I most definitely planned to be totally honest with her, for the simple fact that my lil' lady was out there in the streets and sure could have a co-partner.

The phone rang about three times before someone answered. She answered her self and saved me a whole lot of annoyance. I went ahead and got a precise meeting engagement. It was now a little after four in the afternoon, and by now I was down to my last swallow. I only had a few squares left!

This didn't bother me too much, for I knew that soon enough my ole girl would be knocking on the door with a fresh, new stack. I rather felt sorry for her, because I did tend to mess off a little more than what was necessary and she did put in mostly all the work. Of course, this feeling didn't hold me to act accordingly to our prior relationship! I decided to just leave everything on the table and stretch across the bed until she returned. My reflection in the mirror was as such a slim personage with golden brown complex, sitting upright across the bottom of the bed, with seemingly Chinese eyes, and medium black braided hair.

"She fell for this image," I thought. However, be not deceived! It took hellish game and a little cleverness to shift a chick's gears into motion. A thud or two on the door snatched up all of my attention, instantly!

Don't think I hesitated any to jump up and answer the door. I don't even remember taking steps. It was more of a hand and eye, a twist of the wrist. When she entered, she had a bag in 'er hand about the size of a pack of cigs. She also had some form of liquid in a cup, and I perceived her to be a little tipsy. She also smelled a little like sex! This was all right however, 'cause that's what money smelled like to me in those days!

"Look in the cooler and get ya something. There's a lot of nice things I got for you." I knew she had to keep her energy up and sustain.

I returned to the table myself, for the last gulp, with the cigarette. She had already lain what was made on top of the table as if she couldn't stand having it on 'er. I had no objections to this.

"Are you gonna let me get cha in the bedroom?" I heard her true enough. I responded with what she wanted to hear. I simply lay on back in the bed and after a few minutes of listening to her shower, I fell asleep. She woke me up with her ph.d.! It wouldn't be me if I didn't do the damn thing! So you know the damn thing went down.

Afterwards, I lay looking out the window, and was long gone. There were stormy thunderheads about. I felt religious all of a sudden. I was slick praying for mercy, for I was deep into sin!

I opened my eyes later on that next morning, a little before 9:00 A.M. So that meant we could lay around for maybe another hour or so. That sat quite well with me! The time ahead would be used to formulate other techniques, maybe a few different approaches.

Through my clouded head, I sensed the fact that I had an arrangement later with the other old girl. I felt good about that I suppose. I sort of started to resemble my cousin just a tad. I arose to dress, and then scanned the table seeing the residue of nights past. I wondered if it would resemble it after another hard day's efforts.

I felt selfish as I looked at the swisher sweet cigars; I wanted to take the whole blunt to the head, just me, and the peace of the morning. Many cigars have I broken down and rolled up, and being half way finished, my girl slowly seemed to be waking.

"Hey wus up, love? You got me tired enough to just lie in bed. Ya know that?"

She just lay there with her eyes closed, semi-smiling, with a little leg movement and such. I took a few heavy drags, and I guess she could hear my exhales. I noticed the opening of her deep brown eyes. So the extension of my hand was toward her rising upper body, on to the sitting position, for retrieval of my mini perfectly rolled blunt!

As I sat back to examine the naked top

side of this whore, it looked as if she'd lost about 5 or 10 pounds. It could have been due to all the hours of walking. Be it day or night, warm or cool, we were out there looking for time to tell us if we would succeed, or if we were to fail. If anyone were observing us, they could only bear witness that we were straight up about our business. Sure enough we had bad days, but the very determination of our team meant that most y we were successful.

"Ya see uh, I figured that with all other dates, maybe we should suggest that you contact them again maybe by cell phone, maybe an address, or two." This seemed like it dawned on 'er and at the same time relieved her of maybe hours of unnecessary walking. Making a full exhale of smoke, I got up to look out the window for a weather scope, and peep out the traffic flow.

With it being after 10:00 A.M., our day would be starting soon. Only this time we would start with a better approach! Her motions around the room were showing signs of fitness and flexibility. Her legs looked toned and unbreakable. Her waist and hips were more signatures. If anything, she could only thank me for the collaboration of ours, for when we first met at the corner store in Montebello; she was at least 20 pounds heavier. She didn't have any money sense, and plus the worst of all...the whore was having sex for absolutely free!

The preparation of her hair wasn't too

difficult. It never took long at all. When she was feeling sporty, she hung it in two long ponytail braids and that meant less interference with the clients. Other times she would let it down on all sides, and this seemed to pull in more of a conservative type of clientele.

The blunt was to the end, and thus I gave her the rest whilst I made slight adjustments myself. I had to make sure to grab the room key, and dispose of all incarcerating material! "Nice room," I thought as we exited the confines.

This was the order every time that the lady and I would be checking out of our room. The people that saw us on the parking lot were immediately assuming that me, and some tramp had gotten a room sometime earlier that night, and that I was probably some woman's husband just out for a one-night hit! It didn't trouble me none at all. We actually preferred that perspective of us, than the other of which was definitely incriminating. I couldn't help but notice certain cars, and I do mean specific vehicles. I knew that these guys had to be the cops!

It didn't matter at all, because I didn't have dope on me. I wasn't selling dope. The only thing that could be seen of me was a straight walking, restaurant using, liquor store stopping, cigarette smoking, earphone wearing, pay phone using, young man about his way on the avenue!

There was a welcomed cool mountain pine tree scented breeze at about 10 miles an hour. It didn't last too long. The smoke was soon behind.

You got a three-dollar return when you handed in the remote upon checkout, so I suspect I'd give that change to her for a burger and such at the Dixie Queen a couple of blocks up the avenue.

"Kahlikia, take this and go ahead on up to the spot. I'm uh going to stop over Cuzzo's house for a couple things real fast." Like other times other than this, I had the pleasure of watching a champion female walk off. I had the responsibility of crossing over to the nearest phone, for I personally wasn't planning to be out there too much at all myself. The training wheels that were installed on 'er, were seemingly able to hold 'er up! Besides, some men could notice the connection of us two off top, even if I were two blocks behind her, like that muther-fucking cop!

There was a car on the grocery store lot, across the street. It had an individual in it that didn't fit the descriptions on our agenda! A man that looked as if he weighed at least 300 lbs. was just sitting there on the closest spot along side of the street. The grocery store was at least a full lot away, and at his size, I don't think that he intended on walking across that lot to shop. He wore shaded glasses, and was somewhat baldheaded. For one reason or another, she was close to walking by his car until; the suspect acknowledged that he wanted to talk to her of some sort. I being on the further side, hesitated before attempting to go any closer to this nerve-wrecking article of inconvenience.

Frustration set across my soul, because she knew better than to associate with that type of entanglement. After they talked for at least five minutes, she eventually started off again to the mainstream sidewalk, toward our premeditated action of planning.

I didn't risk it myself, and I wasn't planning to get any closer to her while out there! I was like; it would be another half hour before I hit that sidewalk again. Thinking this over, and being posted up at the closest bus stop, I began lighting a magnificent Newport.

I felt the lose change in my pocket, and I knew it was enough to use the payphone, because right now my full intensions were to get over to ole girl's house and tighten away any lead way to some more money. I thought about what movie would be on as I sat back on her nice and secure couch!

In all honesty, I never meant to cause anyone any harm or misfortune. My only intension was to keep above the waters. In a win or lose situation, it's up to you to choose the right side. This was one of the rules, which we had come to appreciate!

As the bus, that I anxiously awaited, crept up into sight, I gathered the correct change. Then I pulled two to three more times for dispersal of the half-smoked cigarette! It was time to get my thoughts and actions into perspective. Just about an hour ago, I was truly unnerved and shaken up quite a bit. Everyone knows that you gotta accept the bitter with sweet, but I had a weakness for sugar! Upon entrance of the bus, I sat halfway to the back and one seat away from the door. My eyes scanned the horizon for any sign of danger and circumstance. I rather knew that my chances of spotting 'er on the way up the avenue were slim. Either she had gotten to the spot, or she had gotten picked up.

All the same, I knew I wasn't about to get back out there whilst the sun was still up! It didn't take long for me to reach my spot, and upon exiting the bus, I kept in mind to keep my head low and get to the pay phone as fast as possible! The apartment complex was in sight along with the payphone. It had to be no more than two minutes away, and it took me an eternity.

My next move was like an old Atari game, the one with the frog and its determination to cross over to the other side safely. Oh! I was "crunk" about it, strangely enough. I lived for this type of atmosphere! The uncertainty of success was the prime motivator for every move that was being made. I saw a few cars that had some nice looking women. I'd look at them hard, trying to inspire them to either pull over, or turn around! It was somewhat funny. I thought of the idea of being picked up myself, as the whore does! Upon reaching the telephone, all nervousness was cancelled out, by her voice. The new lady was there, indeed! I was simply like, "Open says Me!"

To go see the new lady, I could be seen in the lightweight dress shirt; the baggy, long, dark-blue jeans; and the low top dress shoes. Additionally, I had a set of earphones from time to time. These helped me to have determination to overcome all obstacles.

As I approached the complex, I noticed that on the inside, there was a swimming pool area. The pool had not a drop in it. That appeared strange. The outside of the door had buzzers along side of the door, which meant tenants had to let the visitors in by speaker. Lord knows that made me feel great about knowing that maybe some nights, I'd be there wasted and did not want to be caught off guard!

I chose the middle finger to buzz, for that was exactly how I felt about any uncertain event, therefore preparing me for the bad. But that's the business. She answered, inquired about me, and I entered. After a few seconds of looking around, I perceived it safe enough to make the way to the elevator. All the time, I was hoping that once I had finally made it in 'er home safely, there would at least be some smoking going on!

My ole girl and I had been separated for almost an hour now. I knew that she had at least a couple of condoms left, and a half pack of cigarettes. So she was cool. Plus, she knew that if I was nowhere to be found, she was to return to my kinfolks' apartment, thereby leaving information so I could catch up with her.

She knew to get a room, stay away from strange customers, and she most definitely knew at all times, hold all money in tact! No excuses were necessary.

With the new girl, the intro was as good as gold! She let me know by her way of speaking that there was a place for me in her heart. It may have been lust, curiosity, a game or maybe for romance! But as for me, my plan was to use her for my escape hatch from the flaming trail of a highly misunderstood couple, a couple of breadwinners! I knew that at the end of every night, there must be blunts! There must be good movies!

The elevator door opened on the third floor, and as it opened, I began to exhale! After stepping off the elevator I didn't smell the aroma of say a few dozen wine 'os! So it made me think that this was a fairly decent place. Her apartment was number three, on the left side of the hallway. As I got closer to the door, I could hear an older man's voice, I mean much older than we were. I remember wondering if maybe I had the wrong apartment or something of the sort. I stood there and listened. I was always precautious, and this was extremely new ground for me. I guess she was expecting me, because soon after I knocked, the door was opened.

There was a young boy at about the age of 10 or 11, and I knew instantly that this must have been her son. I spoke and entered along side of this new little person that I probably could bet would end up causing me some sort of mishap, be it him trying to sit up late night with us, or either in the bedroom.

As I entered the main area of the apartment, another person was in sight. I had not seen her and neither did I recognize 'er voice from the telephone. She was a nice looking girl I suppose, and of course in the back of my mind, I already knew that this could pose a problem for sure.

Experience teaches us, that when a man is around sisters, chances were that an unseen atmosphere of tug a war would come to play in give or take a few days! The days and nights of me perhaps coming around would make them a bit more relaxed with the semi-new person's vibe, and liking to my spirit, conversation, and game of choice!

It had been a couple of days or perhaps a week since I'd last seen the new friend of mine. She had changed her hairstyle. I noticed the style of dress that she had also. She sported blue jeans and mostly blue shirts, and if I can recall, I could remember her saying or doing something to give me the assumption that she was maybe "gang related".

"Well, what can I say? We finally got a

little time together. I can't even remember where we left off," I said to her.

"Well, you were telling me about ya hometown, and uh, maybe a couple of things that you find interesting," she said in a go-ahead and continue sort of lyrical tone.

I heard her, and I looked into my heart to select an appropriate re-introduction. I told 'er that I had something to chief on, but that I needed something with which to roll it. She had something for me, and as she left the room in search of it, I looked out the window, slickly looking out for what's er name!

The latest Eminem video was playing on the TV. I had finally gotten settled and patiently waited for her return. I didn't know what to do with my hands and I knew that hand movements were noticed like someone's lips whilst they spoke!

The older fellow sat at the table, and in front of him was a fifth of vodka. I noticed that there were crumb fragments floating around in the bottle. I was thinking, "Damnnnn." His speech was slurred sort of and I noticed that he was trying to communicate to the sisters something about 'what he needed from the store'. When they did speak to him, they spoke other than what you'd expect of any people at least 40 years younger than he was!

"Ya drunk ass! Ya need to go home." Or on another occasion I heard them say "Ya old bastard." Those were the type of sentiments toward this seemingly much older personage.   I tripped off this and it was humorous I suppose.

There was really no furniture other than the couch on which we sat, the kitchen table, and alas the television.

The old person glanced at me from time to time. I was hoping that he wouldn't offer me a drink. I would hate to appear unappreciative.

Outside of the window, out on the lot below, there were men about fixing on a car. Spanish instructions were tossed about, as they perceived different functions that may have needed tended. Tiff, again was back in my sights, and with everything that a man needed. She barely gave me eye contact the whole time, and as I can recall, she had that same characteristic since the first I saw her. She used more of a down scoping, peripheral vision sort of angling. Chilling with 'er didn't necessarily mean we were jabbering every conscious second. We merely passed blunts, laughed at something on TV or either spoke of what we had on the next liquor or beer run!

"Hey, ya talked to my cousin?" I asked. She was like yes, and even they had made plans to go out to the bar later. I thought to myself, this would be a fine time to bring the whole 'sha-bang', to a platter of reality!   As I sat back in thought, the formulations of action ahead were slowly but surely connecting, securing a game plan of a company development. There was no doubt about it, I would be bringing along Kahlikia.

They would come to grips with what I felt was for the good of the whole. Inside, I felt the time was approaching that required me to make moves. There was too much going on! It had me slick smiling.

How does one handle a situation as this? one might ask. What is it about some, and what is it about others, that make the game easy? On the other hand, how do you answer just the opposite, like a rubrics cube? Well in everyday life, one must realize the law of gravity. In order to stay up for movement it took strength and direction. It took mental coordination and balance. It took the five senses of reason. The body and mind had to work together in 'unison' to accomplish whatever it is that was in store. This is the formula to everyday life! It applied to everything that sought substance. Even a parasite has to live up to what it takes to survive; even though it appears that all it does is feed upon its host.

The clothes that I had on were a day old, but the evening was still young. My suitcase was in the closet of my kinfolk's house, so I knew that I would be taking back at least a six-pack. I was excited about the new life of mine, and it surprised me as into how it was being handled. In Memphis, true enough, I had a girlfriend or two, but as far as introduction to such and such - never!

"Hey uh, um bout to bounce! At the same time, I guess I'll see ya later," I said whilst rubbing mine eyes.

"Drinks on me!" she was nodding in agreement, as I began to get up from the security of her couch. On my way to the door I glanced past the old man, but I discreetly looked into the eyes of her older sister. By transaction of expression, we knew that this had better be a neutral relationship.

I was nervous, and this is because she got up herself to walk me to the door! What did she expect from me, a kiss? Well I guess the rain was obvious, but still, I hinted at the fact that I had not seen her bedroom, just to see if she'd bite to see if there were sexual intuitions about!

It was only one o'clock, which was extremely early for us. It meant that I would have to go to another spot for at least another hot four hours! This was no problem, for I only had to jump a couple of fences, and in no time at all, I would be directly in front of where it is that I sought out.

We said our goodbyes for right then. My inner instincts were crying out, "It's party time!"

I took my time as I walked along the sidewalk away from Tiff's house. I had only a few yards before I was at the street's crossing. I was thinking about my new friend actually. From what I could perceive, she didn't appear whorish, but then again, neither did Kahlikia!

What I did know of her was that she moved a little dope occasionally. That was the all too famous 'crack rock'. All the junkies that were seen everyday made me to know that my new friend was most likely getting money!

"I need to focus," I said real low and crispy to myself. Here it was that I was in perfect health, able to work, looking for yet another elevation of labor! I wondered was I ever going to attempt a real job. I did come up to this state to get rid of times past.

There were a couple of stores and a bar at the intersection of the corner. It was close enough to new girl's house, and that of my kin. Chances could be that this would be the place where we were to go later on in the day. I guess it seemed groovy enough!

I increased the speed of my walking. Shhhhiii...business was at hand! The gates were taller than me but that was no issue. It would only take me 8 seconds to jump 'em. The people that noticed me had seen me before a couple of times and I felt they were growing weary of my trespassing.

The way they watched me whilst standing in their doorway made me feel like a prime suspect after a crime had been committed. There was a hole in the fence along side of my folk's apartment. It led out to a path that cut across a yard onto the parking lot of the breakfast shop to which my girl and I had grown attached.

The shop owners recognized me, and I wondered what they could have been thinking. Simple fact, they were the organizers of our food intake! The traffic was constant so every cross over had to be cautiously made. Some of the drivers appeared to be so young in age like they were taking the parent's car out for a spin.

There were always people in line wherever you'd decide to make a stop. This caused slight irritation for me. Wherever my patience went, I have not the slightest Idea. Sure enough, I had made a successful beer run! It had been a day or so since I had last seen 'em (patience), but the beer in hand was accepted as Parle'.

The rocks now replaced the soil by which the lot had formerly been covered. It made ya stepping slowly and sluggishly. Plus with each step, you could hear the sound effects of rocks being kicked about. There was an apartment up from kinfolk's, and there were Asians that had residence. They usually were playing the game. They had a weed pipe and sometimes they were generous. I just threw the peace sign at 'em on my way up to the apartment. I could hear people in the inside talking about something tied in with laughs in between. This atmosphere was best to enter upon. It was more relaxing, and the feelings of intrusion were non-existent.

"Deuce," my cousin's husband opened the door for me. "Hey, wus up Kutty!"

After our fellowship salute, he informed me that Kahlikia was sitting at the kitchen table.

"Cuzzo, go ahead and set those in the

freezer. We got some out front."

I turned the attention to the insiders with another salute. Quickly, I made way past them and into the kitchen, not a second too soon. I had been carrying that beer for the longest time it felt.

To my surprise, she was on the telephone. There was no need to interrupt for I knew she was arrancing maybe one of the dates that we planned upon earlier. I stood behind 'er and felt proud shall I say of her performances! She'd shown me that she was willing.

The second day after the first day we met, I do recall her telling me that the situation with us, would be a lasting one! Taking a seat at the table, sitting back listening to 'er chop 'em up gave me mental ease and stabilization, for most of the walking could be cut as much as fifty percent.

She held a piece of paper in 'er hand. It had at least three numbers on it. A couple of 'em seemed to be Hispanic. I'd be willing to bet someone that before the sun rose again on the next day, I would at least twist another twelve tops from the different beer or alcoholic beverages, beginning with the one in hand!

Truly in a spirit to celebrate, I needed to pick out some clothes, shave, shower, get my hair situated, get a room, re-up on necessities, and most importantly, get her ready as well.

"Hey Cuz, I talked to home-girl Tiff. She said that they'd be over in a lil-bit!"

After Rochelle told me the news it was a boost to my spirits! Kahlikia made her entrance into the room with us. She took her seat beside me. The vibes settled down around us. The night's planning was in due process. We had officially moved on to the next gear!

My cousin Rochelle suddenly notified my girl about a dress or two that maybe would suit her. Soon after, they arose and proceeded to the bedroom with mini-chat-girl stuff on the way down the hall.

Deuce and I just sat around on the couch lighting and extinguishing Kools and Newports. We were two normal young men but, with marvelous women! We were hunters when the time called for it, which with us was every other week or so.

In fact the gleam of desire had set in for yet another masquerade! They came back to the front after about an hour. Then lo and behold, it was damn near suppertime.

CHAPTER 12:
WORST-CASE SCENARIO

Tlzz was September 23 2003, 7:27 P.M. With the smoke of two substances clouding my vision, in hand was one, partially finished beer. Also at my side was a very unique individual that caused the worst-case scenario in another's household. This was the very enemy to a wife's so-called control over her man as far as the sexual connection of the two was concerned. Kahlikia wasn't a mean-spirited person at all, nor was she dirty, but what she represented to some was a primetime event after merciless days of drought from one's man or woman.

She was a twenty-minute or less escape from whatever it may have been for the individual at hand. I looked at 'er for a few seconds without her knowledge of it; just scoping what it was that had developed this young lovely lady Into a fearless money pursuer! Picking up the phone, I noticed she rather had a concern as into what I was getting at by that call of action. She herself was as such; and I knew that if another woman had entered the picture, she would be expected as well, to contribute to the well being of another tomorrow! Never the less, with a glance, wink, and a tap on the thigh, she felt then that it was all for the good!

"Hey, uh, wus up? We 'bout to leave out. Just calling seeing what the time might be!" I never spoke on the phone for more than what was required.

It was time for me to prepare, for the women were on key, and in a few minutes, Tiffany would be pulling up maybe even that sister of hers as well. The suitcase that lay on the closet floor was laid across the bed for tonight's exquisite unleashing. I chose a black short sleeve shirt, with some tan khaki pants, with the low top Polo shoes, brown in color. The style of my hair would come up out of the braids I had, for now it was decided that the hair was to be pressed and straightened out before curling. I wondered, but then again who was I to judge!

My dreams were intense on me as I slept during the night sometimes. They had violent endings to what some could say would be the outcome in this life that I lived. The women that were now a part of one's dealings could be said to account for most of one's tragedy, for envy, jealousy, and hate gathered in the hearts of men as they grew to know me and those Memphis' ways of mine.

They may have had ties to other men, and this I sweated none the least. My ears were in the front with the others while my body sat there with only half the hair done.

"Hey love, how ya feeling?" I asked as my hand automatically began the sequence of the "smoketh of thou" cigarette.

She spoke with low tones and a classical expression, maybe it was the new look she had that enlightened her for I damn near was getting sweaty, or maybe it was the pressing comb. My cousin's husband "Deuce" had a time on his hands balancing the different elements that surrounded their home on almost, a daily level! His hair was longer than mine. This motivated me to never, ever cut my hair.

"Hey, Cuz, we gonna run to the liquor store. Ya want something?" Reaching into my pocket was cool though. A young dude was feeling a bit secure.

The beverage cost about seven dollars for we would be drinking Tequila now. After receiving the drink money, out the door he was, with the Denver Broncos hat, and a light windbreaker. How his wife dealt with the women that came around us was beyond me!

With the examples of my cousin Mac J. and me, one must say that they had a hell of a bond! Lighting the cigarette and handing it to my girl, those simple things alone weren't anything other than game. Getting use to something touching on my neck with a tickling sensation would take a second or two. Once she was finished, my hair laid flat all the way around. It lay flat against my head and down part of my neck. This was the first stage. Soon after, there would come the curling. I needed a break before she began on the next phase of her selected hair-do.

So in the front room we sat amongst the company, being my cousin, my old girl, and then on another note, my newest friend Tiffany. Her sister was there as well. Hey, the more the merrier they say!

The eyes of each of us shifted around. We looked into each other's eyes for the understanding of the night's coming. We searched spirit and observed the talk any signature of being wasted early was a real no-no! Filled with the fire of life, all of us seemed to be on the further side of the night, ready to kick it.

How would this be possible? I wasn't rich. Neither was I the best-looking man on the planet. So inside there was a slight shadow of uncertainty! This lasted all the way up to the point to where my partner, my cousin's husband made it back, and of course in hand my half pint of Jose Tequila.

Now it didn't faze me as how many cups were gathered to have their shot. This was never a debate! We smoked together and we all most definitely drank together. At the same time, my calculations of each pouring let them know that I did intend to drink most of it. Could someone honestly blame me?

"What time y'all, we gonna be heading out?" my new lil' lady friend asked the room. To us, that was an unanswerable question for only straight absoluteness, got us to stepping out the door. But, the sound of those words did trigger a slight premonition for exit sometime in the next hour. There was only the curling to finish up. I personally was feeling as if I could wear it as it was but sporting the curls wouldn't be so bad. Once seated again I sat still. The curling irons kind of made me drift off in thought!

If I could quote someone in the music industry, it would be "Playa Fly" when he said, "Love 2 hate me. Motivate me!" I swear I could understand his words in all sincerity at this stage, at this particular point in living. I had never curled my hair before as this, and it rather made me look like a totally different human being.

Both of the girls were giving me the "It's going to be you and me" type of look! It may have gone that way the same night as far as another guy was concerned. Don't get me wrong, I was truly human. The same tendencies existed, but the pursuit of clientele was the bottom bases for this outing of ours.

Everyone now was dressed, meaning

we all got up and stepped outside into the clearness of the night sky. The air was so sweet. It was like the mountains were breathing. With each exhale, gushes of pine tree-scented breeze struck us, with ever so needed breaks from the toxic smoke with which we mostly overloaded ourselves.

There was no need to use any vehicles, for Thrust's Bar was only a couple blocks away. That my dear friends, suited us alcoholics just fine! Kahlikia and I lagged behind as we walked for there was strategy to discuss, and inconvenience if any to iron out.

"So I see you got a couple of numbers. Did anyone inquire about a date? Well tonight I want you to mingle with the gentlemen. Chances are that you'll strike it up with someone! I mean you looking good on the real though."

The way she looked at me next, was something more for at her glance I felt slickly. "Is there a chance that um in over my head?"

All eyes were on us as we made our ways through the front door of the bar. Immediately we were in front of the bartender, ordering a few rounds of the coldest beer. Deuce and I, after establishing a table, made our ways to the pool table, giving the women a chance to settle down, to mingle in with the others that were there celebrating.

I saw my old girl beginning her trade. She observed the men, waved to some, and began a conversation with another, all at the same time! I knew that Tiff was at it too, but her trade of choice looking at the strange lady that she was dealing with, I knew that transactions of some kind would eventually come about.

"Rack 'em up Cuz." I did. This was a game I was growing to like. The more it was played, I was the loser, but then again I felt my skills enhancing. At times, it was like I was a little competition instead of just a clean wipe out. There were a few women around other than our own dates and this fish was intending on taking the bait full fold if some women gave me a glance that lasted over three seconds. I had nothing to lose, but anything to gain!

My southern accent heightened my success rate so to speak for only after the first few words, there would be the question of 'where is it that I come from', 'what part of the country, and if I intended on staying awhile'?

"I'll be right back Cuz." Then he walked off to see about his wife and all the chairs around me remained unoccupied, for this fellow wasn't planning on what ifs. This was more like what it was going to be!

The lady that seemed to be interested, sat across from the table, from whereas we were playing our game. She didn't seem intimidated by my stepping up to her. Being calm with it, I simply said hello! I told her that I would be here for a while if she wanted to talk or perhaps a drink.

Well ole girl had some guy spell bound!

I'd bet that he could of never thought that she and I were connected. We were playing it so coollllll! We kept in mind not to be seen the least as far as sitting together in conversation. That would be shaking up the would-be client! That could not be chanced!

These individuals were very necessary to our livelihood! These were the ones who provided us with what it took to get by on the next day. Meanwhile, Tiff sat with Lachelle behind a haze of cigarette smoke! Did I mention the cigarette smoke and half-empty pitchers of beer.

Tiff had her eye on me and I noticed from time to time, there was no problem with this, or whatever we chose to do whilst in the place, for she got hers on. That was a whole 'nother tip.

After leaving out the restroom, I went ahead and took a seat with those of whom I came to the bar with minus ole girl of course.

"Wus up Tiff? What cha drinking on?" After that I took it upon myself to taste for myself. This was no problem for her, for I was thinking she liked the attention, and in no way did I want her to think that she was being ignored, none the least!

Kahlikia was chopping 'em up good! That gave me the nonchalantly time, to take another sip from Tiff's small shot of Tequila! With squinted eyes I scoped the Joe that looked like he would eventually be contributing to our next meal.

Inside of me, the fire of triumph began to burn brightly! "How about tomorrow you and I spend some real time together. Perhaps I could stay over the night?". Her response was well intact with what I felt was going on inside her street little mind from the jump!

"Cuz, how about another game?" He took another gulp from his glass, then both of us got up to head back over to the pool area. Before though, I made it my business to go up to the bar for a shot of Tequila, and to pass the spirit of notice ability to my old girl. She knew it, for I saw her signal that she had gotten another one! and um thinking there was really no need to take the small glass over to the table. For in one gulp it was easily finished! With a side-glance at the new couple {per-say}, I made my way on over to the game at hand, feeling as if I had a chance to maybe win for once!

My cousin Lachelle was a straight player. This one couldn't deny! Every word and even her body language was pure. This you could only understand I guess from actually knowing her. She had perfect teeth and two side golds, one on each side. I thought over my walking ability, being careful not to lose cool points 'cause there was no need to rush, for I most certainly was somewhat tipsy!

The outfit that hung loosely on my 140-pound frame looked as if I were walking against a windstorm with slow strides and parallel sights, using more peripheral vision than natural sight, and more sound dependency than that of touch!

If anyone were watching me, it could be easily understood how I could be highly underestimated. The inner power and rage that pumped through the blood and flesh of my structure was highly compact, and well camouflaged!

Back in my hometown, this scenario would be highly ridiculed, and the truth would sound like nothing more than someone's fantasy! It was funny to me at times, when I wanted to call down just to chop it up with familiar spirits, but then I wondered why spoil a good thing?

This was the kind of thing that was only heard on the silver screen. No way could they accept that the semi-junky that they last saw, was well into what it is that most young men were dreaming about!

The music in the club that was playing wasn't exactly the dancing music. There was country, and a little rock! There was no R&B, nor Rap music. I don't even recall hearing the mighty R-Kelly. So the mode and events of a man and the young lady was strictly by conversation.

The balls were racked into their triangular shape for the breaking, and even though my attempts were vain, Duce had sympathy giving me the option of break! The gesture that meant maybe I'd get lucky with a few fall ins, thereby giving me a small lead. Looking down my stick, I slid it back and forward trying to power up for a straight hit. Lo-and behold two balls actually fell into the hole.

The night was getting late, and the ties of the end were coming together evenly. It was time to pull on the poles and see what we had on hook. Would it be a brim, a catfish, a bass, maybe trout or tuna and a possibility of crab.

One thing for sure was a net could pretty much pull up the whole platter. But that would take months to develop and dealing with just two or three poles would mean that you only had those options. That didn't set in too well with us!

Mac J., on the other hand, had a major net! It came in the technique of the computer age. The online service, the means by which to progress across this grand land of opportunity! For most beginners, the pavement and side streets were your opportunities to excel. Paying dues meant that whatever was made, there was no option of splurging and having loose pockets. All ends that came in were specifically used for the foundation of the nights!

Kahlikia and the older gentlemen that sat with 'er were now looking as if they were intending to leave. My heart rate started up, for I didn't know if they were going to his house, or across the street to a room, or just maybe, in the alley out back! One thing was for certain, there would be money as the outcome of whatever the plan of choice it would be between them, and this was for damn sure!

The other three were probably hip to what was going on. It did not matter if I had been daydreaming, talking to others, or stepping outside the bar for any old reason, they understood it was good for my success and theirs. We all would dip bread in the gravy. Therefore, letting strangers get next to one of us went on always under supervision...totally.

At this point if I were in a relationship with 'er, now was usually the time to walk over and inquire about the goings about of the fellow and all. Being jealous, but no the pool game was getting good! There were three solid balls and four stripes left on the table. Looking at my buzz, as he stood on the other side squinting at the play at hand, I knew that we had a game.

Kahlikia, as she walked toward the door, motioned that they'd be right back. My attention was on this mutherfucking shot! After another loss in pool, it being as close as it were, all the drinking and etc, started to show it's wearing on us all It was time to begin our departures. My girl was back now, she had just made it not even eight minutes ago!

There weren't too many other picks about. Thus, the remaining part at the bottom of the pitcher was untouched. We all sat together for the next few minutes soaking up the fact that we had a small walk ahead of us. If I should say so myself, we damn near needed a taxi! Tiffany was all right though, for her apartment was no more than a block away. In my heart I knew that if it was just I alone, that it probably would have been my next stop for the night. But there was business to attend to though, for the money that ole girl had just made wasn't necessarily accounted for at the moment!

"Well y'all, what cha think?" my cousin set out on us. I looked for my lighter. Tiff sat there examining her nails. Deuce had his attention on the couple of people left that sat at the bar, while Kahlikia sat beside me with her leg damn near in the spot where my leg was resting. I guess she was somewhat insecure as to who I would be having sex with!

How is this dealt with? 'Cause for damn sure, you would have to have me completely and most certainly, (fucked UP!). Well, as for me, the decision was rather an easy one to make. My new girl, I couldn't really blame her, for maybe she didn't understand like she should have. Maybe she felt like eventually maybe I'd come live with her, go to the movies, lie down at night, and whisper sweet things in her ear!

You probably could guess what it is that I truly had in mind. Don't get me wrong, those things were in the future to come, and as I counted the collected money, I knew that it would be in the distant future, maybe a couple of decades or so.

It didn't make any difference to me, one way, or the other. I practically could lie with both, but not to push it though for they were still timid about the game!

Sure enough, I felt pressurized by this strange inconvenient, but lovely entourage of two women! What would the liquor make me do? In my mind, I was unable to calculate any reasonable outcome.

Somewhat quiet, she became. I wondered if Kahlikia was feeling used and abused. Was she having second thoughts as in how her life was going? Looking at 'er in the moonlight, it seemed like her thoughts were displaying neon flags for attention!

Frustration was never too far off from me, I was feeling instead that she should be thankful for not having to ask anyone for anything: no food, no weed, not a cigarette, nor shelter from the night, transportation - the silly whore!

The next morning we had to see about fixing a truck. The truck was old. It was really put together (so to speak). Sections of it were damaged nearly to the point of non-repair. The engine was the key! Be it not a reflection of the motor, for the motor could haul up to a thousand pounds!

The engine sounded almost as good as a 5.0 Mustang if ya weren't aware! We heard its engine many nights as my lil' cousin Tack and I lay as shiftless as we could about the bed of the thirty-five year old truck. The turning in and off the many cuts had us sliding around always seeking a better grasp of something not covered by oil nor mud. We sought rims, transmissions, Cadillac converters, the back end of pick-up trucks, whatever it may have been, and it usually would suffice as a structure to lie on top of until it was lying amongst the other items at our stash spot.

"Man Cuz, we gonna get a half when we finish up tonight?" I agreed to this 'cause I liked kicking it with my lil' cousin when I could.

The dirt and oil would cover my clothes for sure and this was for sure! They weren't having any mercy at all when It came to making left or right turns.

'Allen Den' was his name. He spoke with a country accent. His choice of music was straight country! This took some getting use to.

"Hey y'all, we'll let you two out," were his instructions to my cousin and me.

"All get down in those bushes. We gonna pull out to the side - kind of in the back part of the fence."

Then again, it was really somewhat unoccupied therefore making it a grand opportunity for us to get through the fence to snatch every transmission, carburetor engine block whatever was in sight.

We were naturally hyped up about the event at hand. It was better than looking elsewhere. It cut the anticipation down tremendously, the anticipation to kick it! The four of us were to the extreme! We had no limits. We had no fear. We only had determination.

We only looked ahead to the ending achievement to what ever it was that was in reachable means. Tack's girl, knew my girl. They had been hanging out for a few days now. She had her own apartment and that was one hell of a relief on a niggard pockets fan show!

For only a couple of weeks ago, it was just us. Time had passed and thank God, we had survived so far. The scales were changing also. Tizz new levels of dealing ships had arisen. Now a day's I and my girl had taken refuge at 'er apartment. Her name was Lexus. She had a three-year old daughter as well.

My girl and I had started to camp out because of the simple fact the police and under-covers began to show signs of interest in our affairs about the avenue - as if they didn't know.

With the theme music blasting silently in our heads we climbed to the back, and out up the back bed of the truck door, keeping our heads and shoulders low as we crept into the yard, and low into the high grass that dotted the yard.

Seeing each other, but at the same time listening and watching for any kindred moment of incarceration, making us all the more stealth in movement! Hearing the insects, you could distinguish at least three or four different squeaking, chirping, or hissing sounds in the air, like a watch, but with the sounds of nature, instead of ticking!

When the time was right, we crept into the fence and over to the other side of the junkyard. The technique was simple - grab all major structures - any thing mechanical, and all lesser appliances if there were any in sight.

Walking cautiously over the area, we managed to grab a couple of engine blocks! There were a couple of carburetors, and a couple more things that I couldn't identify.

Twenty-five minutes had passed since the load of the truck came to an ease before stopping. Instantly we started making way to the exit, fully intending on getting away from this steaming payload.

"In the morning, we'll cash the rest of this stuff in," he told us. After another minute standing there amongst each other, looking crazy, we were each off into the next stage of our nights. Tack and I decided to walk over to the Nome Apartmen Complex after we stopped over his homeboy's house, maybe to sit over there on the steps of the second floor, and stare out over the city night-lights drinking, smoking, and preparing for the newest freestyle session.

"Cuz, you got some extra condoms?" he asked me, whilst I was getting comfortable after that fifteen minute walk. I told him that the ones I had left were for the chick, and that I stood a chance of missing a hundred dollars by not having it when they were needed. But what the hell, I thought taking out the condom from pocket 3, it was handed over to the appreciating you chap!

Caught up in the steady flow of the night traffic, I immediately regained my senses in the form of craving. "Now roll that blunt, Cuz!" I playfully chanted up to 'em, dropping a couple of verses tuning us up as for the mini-studio session.

In my mind I was kicking my own ass, for letting that 100-dollar ticket go for nothing other than a younger fellow's horny intentions toward a 40% to 60% chick. It's a strange sensation to relax and have everything you desire present.

You almost feel as if things were going too smoothly, and you expected something misfortunate! This is how the dice rolls though. Since we had no instruments, our options were centered on the food to live, principles, and the law of sustenance is self-preservation first!

A halfway finished bottle and a newly rolled blunt had us sitting straight enough for the remainder of the evening. Off and on I would daydream about what tomorrow would be like, an interruption byway of incoming blunt passages between the two of us. In all, it was getting back to the broad that kept me from going to sleep. Tiredness was showing its wings.

On our way back to the apartment of the girlfriend of my cousin, we talked about some deep down south material. The late night block walks, the late day awakenings, the midday boredom! Everything was on the chart of discussion being one hundred percent to every memory we could manage to bring to light. He had an older girl at least 10 years than he, better proven than said, he mostly got around to having it mostly to his advantage.

Her old school Cadillac was at his discretion, along with the amount of time we would be missing in action! For when he and I got behind the wheel, all bets where off.

If I were to speak words that I held to myself while in the passenger seat, they would have sounded like rap songs on the radio that had the beeping sound as word placement!!!!! I kept in my mind the whole time, damn! Don't ever get in the car with this man again! He had me clutching the seat for dear life, not to mention when he chose to use a side alley road, the ones made of gravel instead of pavement.

The expressway during almost daybreak, were curves slick with the moisture of approaching dew! My heart rate was about the same as the engine, if not louder. I was like "Hurry up and park this muther-fucker!"

The looks that he gave me were nonchalant as into how I felt about his speed obsession. When dealing with an under age individual, ya had to be careful not to frustrate them, especially while they were behind the wheel!

The fifteen-minute ride to the grocery store cost me at least three cigarettes, and once in park, I fired up another one. He got out the car to approach one of whom he'd spoken to earlier that had been posted awaiting our arrival. After three minutes he came back, and after starting the car for the ball off, looked at 'em again but this time having no other choice but to convey my feelings.

"Hey Cuz, You got me nervous as hell. Please get us back safely, for me though Cuz!" He eased off gently making me feel good about the relaxing ride back. So Far it seemed cool enough.

"We had no other intensions, besides getting back to the spot maybe to watch a few minutes of TV, listen to some music perhaps. Our Uncle Allen Den was there when we arrived. He had been on a smoking spree and we were just in time to see him, and all the drama that his fiery soul could deliver. Off sight there was his signature bushy beard, wildish eyebrows, and slick curly hair. Upon seeing him you couldn't tell if this was just the beginning, or was it the end of his night? I loved him with a deep respect, for he was outlawed as far as human passions were found, for mostly everyone that knew/him, knew of his Memphis.

"Y'all ruthlessness lifestyle. He too was originally from [be ready in the morning?" he said to us while standing in the doorway.

We certified him that we'd be up early,no doubt we always sought another plan of action to qualify a grand night! Tack and I smoked ourselves into a cloud and almost quietly, listened to those two whores gossip about their premeditated schemes. We only sat back with the expression of many hands make lighter work on our faces..

There was no checkout time. This we had to be cautious of for we would tend to want to only sit back, roll blunts, and watch TV. It was cool though, she had contacted a trick or two by telephone, and one of them was a guarantee the time and pick up had already been arranged, so that was another hundred dollars we could collect for ourselves!

The fact was, my uncle Allenden didn't want to be disturbed so early in the day, and really this was all good with us.

The little girl of the house sat before the television watching the cartoons of today's age, and man I thought how the animation had changed!

Tack and his girl were at the table doing what they do best. My girl, she was walking about feeling good about the fact that the telephone was her gleaming white knight, rescuing her tender feet from the drive and determination of her man!

Looking into the refrigerator, there were steaks, and a few other things that would combine into a fine dinner for the evening.

Alexus was on the telephone with a girl. She was about our age, and she was Hispanic. Boy was I interested!

"Hey, let me talk to 'er," I asked her. After a few more words or so she handed me the phone. Turns out that she was in need of a spot, for her man was kicking her ass out the house! Boy! when it rains, it pours.

Alexus was acceptable and sympathetic to 'er cry. I would be walking to a bus stop to meet 'er and accompany her back to the hide away of ours!

Excitements...panic...suspicion...glee... joy...radiated me. Kahlikia was to be leaving out for 'er date in another half hour which would give me the necessary time and space to do what I seemed to do best!

I'd call Tiffany, maybe see what she was smoking. Then again, I could just walk right across the street. I felt like I was sort of neglecting her and thangs!

My footsteps could be heard as I dotted my way outside onto the sidewalk. I was on my way to the upcoming guest of the highest anticipation! I had never had any nationality other than black women, so, you could imagine my structure of mind. Would I talk to 'er black, or would I be semi other for the sake of purity?

On down Peoria, I then saw the first of what looked to be her! There was a suitcase in one hand and on the other arm, a backpack of some kind.

I saw long hair moving with the current

of wind, and with the personality of her walk. Closer we got, and upon face-to-face encounter, I reached to take away one of the bags that had her petite body out of context to what it really was.

Her language was marvelously accented with her Spanish of course, I damn near was ready to pass out. I looked at 'er like damn, how many ways can a motherfuckah get down!

"So, you and I are going to be under the same roof day and night. How will I be able to contain myself?" I said jokingly.

"Well, I just got out of a bad relationship, and now I just wanna chill out, relax myself," she said.

All the time, I was already picturing what it would be like once the lights were low, and the drugs and alcohol had fully relaxed us, not to say that I needed them or anything like that, but it was going to be the case as far as I saw it. On another dial, how would the truth of me and my other friends strike her?.

Oh, I wasn't eager to let 'er in on the one she would come to know as T.H. so I decided otherwise. She would see soon enough! We were back at the apartment after ten minutes of walking, or should I say, strolling down the avenue. She burst into that sweet language of hers to Alexus, and a few hugs of appreciation. It was cool as far as Alexus was concerned, because this dear girl was a manager at McDonald's meaning she automatically was going to be a contribution. I sat down to calm myself, and looked proudly upon this day and time of mine!

Later on that night, I was lying about then, lo and behold she was back from her mini celebration of being single. It appeared as if she had gotten wasted during the process!

"Hey, wus up?" she said to me with those dark squinted, twinkling eyes, the eyes of a rapist if I were to describe them properly. This bothered me none the least.

I was somewhat shook-up. I can't lie! We were really close. I mean not even one-foot's distance. Alexus was laid out on the floor supposedly sleep. Facing our immediate direction, the sneaky bitch seemingly was about to turn into one of those xxx rated programs, live, and in living color!

Alikia was in the backroom asleep, deservingly so. As we were into each other's arms, I held back! The kisses she was laying on me were deep kisses at that! She most definitely was on fire! The pants that she wore were soaked like someone had wasted a cup of water into her lap. I pulled away then again. I pulled even further apart from her, because I knew she had been drinking. That disturbed my conscience.

I didn't want her to wake up and feel as if she were drunk and were taken advantage of, so I downplayed the situation until she realized that I wouldn't undress. Slowly but surely though, she eased up in 'er wanting, and sat or lay down on the floor for the sleeping stage of the after-effects of alcohol.

I hated my decision to not have sex with her, but I felt it was a wiser thing not to go at this particular time anyhow. Running my fingers along the side of her tannish, gold face and hair, I passionately stroked the sides of 'er head and waist. I could smell the liquor with her breathing.

Looking across at Alexus, I felt that maybe she was awake, and maybe disappointed, really I thought, if I would have had an extra condom, chances were that she would have probably got it! I smelled like her perfume, her scent was on my person, and being that close to each other, it was amazing that I didn't have any other residue of the night's passing!

There were three female voices to distinguish three more personalities to translate but then, I still had one perception of the three-sided dilemma. It had been forever since it last rained. I kind of remembered the slight snowfall, but trying to recollect the last shower was far from me.

It wasn't just real hot, but at times I'd still want to listen to the rain, just to forget the game for a while. To be a normal person not trying to get something, to straight chill, not paying as much attention to the women and everything!

Our Hispanic friend's name was Lisa, and on her left wrist were the letters L.C.C. I was curious as to what it stood for. Statistically speaking, there weren't too many young black men my age around. The time that we originally left Colorado, was when I was the age of five. Thus the years down south maybe separated my person from the almost extinct generation that most certainly would have been my peers!

Everyone was up and in action about today. To be honest, I just let the natural sequence of my original girl and I roll over to what was immediately...apparent...for never was I to trade one true one, for one that hadn't been tested. Kahlikia sat close to me and I didn't give too much concern as into what she may have felt about our ties together.

There really was no hoping for any type of relationship in our worlds. It seemed to be only business.

"I got to go later on, me and Mac J, gonna hit the town and maybe a couple of clubs. Maybe you and the girls will have a little while to get with each other." Alikia caught every word, with her fullest attention.

"Ya gonna bring something back for later?" she asked. I told 'er that she could expect nothing more than my return, meaning it was on them to get straight, and considering that it was three of 'em, I figured they'd be all right!

The sooner he got there the better, because honestly I preferred being around other elements of this grand city, plus it was early in the evening thereby plenty of daylight was left. We would be clean and it was nice to be seen. Lisa was now about her way getting prepared for work, putting on her uniform and taking care of some last minute detail of her makeup. When we looked at each other there was definitely something different in those glances. Did she not like the fact that I declined sex? Did it bother her? Was it just my early perception of yet another project to unfold?. As I walked to the back room to check on 'er frame of mind, I only stood to examine her movements. They were quick and halfhearted.

"You off to work? Make sure you save some of that there energy for me o-k." She listened and kept about her hair, releasing a kind of irritated exhaling sound. Therefore this started making me to think I'd need a chisel and hammer to knock away the impediments that clouded her understanding of me!

There was a knock on the door and I was sure it had to be my Cuz, Mac J. I could tell by the nonchalant tap on the door that the door was not worthy. Happily I grabbed my shades whilst opening the door and after speaking to each other we started our walk off to one of the cars he drove. This time it was the four door white Cadillac Fleetwood, and man it moved like an airplane. It sounded like a well-tuned boat!

Immediately getting settled, after a couple of blocks, the indo smoke was in the air, and mixing us in to the levels of the mode, the pimp's mind. Next was the store for a case of beer. While I sat in the car awaiting his return, something dawned on me. It had taken him like 20 years to establish his estate, so how long would it take me with all of the ups and downs, the police harassment, the chances of catching a disease, losing women? I considered really all of the above. What was worst I felt, would be - never really knowing what love and a relationship with a real woman was like. Man what a thought!

The first two beers we popped were just the icebreakers. We had intended on getting fully loaded, and the fact that we were blood related made the vibes all together clear and untainted by the years that have past us. He damn near was my babysitter before we left, and even then I could remember there was always a female around, and if I can recall at that time, I rather remember him in a relationship. That must have been one of the last before all of that was finished.

The last of the joint was beginning to heat up my thumb and first finger, but it was some pure, so I wasn't too quick to part with it. The day was beautiful, and always complimented by those fantastic bluish grey and snow tipped mountains from one side of the horizon to the other.

The clouds were torn apart as they made their way to the different destinations of that most fantastically blue sky. From time to time you'd see hang gliders. They would be the size of a speck, but you knew what they were, as in the circle motions of their flight.

"So how you and ya old girl doing Cuz? Y'all managing pretty well I see. But I'm uh telling ya, it takes more than getting up and out here everyday. It takes will power and tolerance for this bullshit! See, a whore makes you rich, or a bitch can get cha broke. Know what I mean Cuz? If you fall weak for a whore, then she becomes the bitch."

I sat there damn near motionless, soaking up all the vitamins I felt my soul needed to maintain a devious enchamberment that I was referring to as a means to surviving.

The first spot he pulled up on was somewhat huge being a pool hall and all. Upon entering, there were things that could be done to shake two hard working men like us into an enlightening occasion. Barely paying attention to the women, Cuz, and I began the first game of pool. Over to our immediate right, there seemed to be a double date going on, two girls and two boys. We also noticed the pressure that he and I caused the fellows to be under. All this by just our being around - what a shame.

About the Author and the Artist

Terry Holt

The Author

I can't say that going through this life of mine has been easy. It's been far from that. I have ambitions that are somewhat far-fetched. That's what other people say though. In this opportunity, I sincerely hope to reach as many people as one can.

The books that are on the way are not the average. Through the use of different emotional frequencies, I think that the reader might find it not hard to stay centered. Maybe these books will lift you. Maybe they will make you laugh. I just hope that I've at least entertained one's sense of "getting away" from it all.

The Artist

The art that you may have seen comes from being in constant atmospheres that are either too dangerous to relax properly, or on another note, too joyful to sit over extended periods of time. The pictures start with light lead. Afterward comes an intensely supervised microscopic ink stretch-out.

Since I've been with the colors, my pictures have taken on new dimensions. As if you would have to touch it to see where the surface started. These images take lots of time to shape. Some of them completely absorb me - taking my strictest attention. I only pray that the people that may have interest, would take the many minutes necessary to examine every centimeter. In doing so, you'll see me there as well – just my way of waving hello!